Dinah Maria Mulock Craik

Sermons out of Church

Dinah Maria Mulock Craik

Sermons out of Church

ISBN/EAN: 9783741123160

Manufactured in Europe, USA, Canada, Australia, Japa

Cover: Foto ©Andreas Hilbeck / pixelio.de

Manufactured and distributed by brebook publishing software
(www.brebook.com)

Dinah Maria Mulock Craik

Sermons out of Church

SERMONS OUT OF CHURCH

BY THE AUTHOR OF

"JOHN HALIFAX, GENTLEMAN"

"Thy will be done on earth as it is in heaven."

,

LONDON

DALDY, ISBISTER, & CO.

56, LUDGATE HILL

1875

CONTENTS.

———

Sermon I.

WHAT IS SELF-SACRIFICE?

WHAT IS SELF-SACRIFICE?

I LATELY saw a drawing, not unknown to archæologists, which, though it might shock some people as painfully profane, struck me with just the contrary feeling, as being a solemn and touching confirmation, from the outside, of that internal truth which we call Revelation. It was a copy of a street caricature, found, not very long ago, on a newly discovered wall—I think in Rome—where it had been hidden for eighteen hundred years ;—evidently the work of some young *gamin* of the ancient world, and depicting a man, after the most primitive style of Art, with a round O for his head, an oblong O for his body, two lines for legs and arms, and five rayed fans for hands and feet. This creature stood gazing in adoration upon a similar man, only with an ass's head instead of a human one, who hung suspended upon a cross. Underneath was scrawled, in rude Greek letters, "*Alexaminos worships his God.*"

It set me thinking. "Alexaminos worships his god." Not God, mind you, but *his* god; the divinity of his own making, with an ass's head on. How many excellent and earnest-minded people do much the same!

To pull the ass's head off—to show how many a ridiculous idol is esteemed divine; how often a so-called virtue is in reality a vice, or slowly corrupting into one; how the sublimest and holiest truths may be travestied into actual lies—this is the aim of my Sermons out of Church. Out of Church : outside each and all of those numerous and endlessly diversified creeds preached in buildings made with hands; but not, I hope, outside of that universal Church— God's consecrated Temple—built without hands, " eternal in the heavens."

Is this iconoclasm ? I cannot think so. Is it irreligious ? Surely not; to those who believe that the heart of all religion lies in the words I have put on my title-page, "Thy will be done on earth as it is in heaven." But to find out what that will is, and—so far as the finite may comprehend the infinite—Him who declares it, this, and this alone, is real Christianity.

Let me begin "at the very beginning," as children say—children, in their holy ignorance, often so much wiser and nearer heaven than we.

In first planning this first sermon, I entitled it "The Sin of Self-sacrifice;" because I have noticed, as one of the sad and strange things in life, what folly, what misery, what actual wickedness, result from the exaggeration of this particular virtue, esteemed the highest of all, the very key-stone and crown of our faith. But considering the point, and feeling that such a title might startle weaker brethren, and give an impression that I meant what I do not mean, and that my Sermons out of Church are also out of the pale of all Christianity, I have abstained, and simply commence with the open question—What is self-sacrifice?

The most obvious answer is this. Self-sacrifice means the sacrifice of one's self, one's personal ego, with its aims and desires, to something or somebody else. Then, in this transaction, is the most important element the self which is sacrificed, or the object which it is sacrificed to? In other words, granted that self-sacrifice is a good thing, which side is to reap the good? Or is there to be a third consideration, more important than either—its end and aim? And what is its end and aim?

A moralist might answer, "Absolute truth, absolute right." A Christian, knowing how difficult it is to define either, might reply, "God;" which involves three necessities—the comprehension of Him, the worship of Him, and the duty and delight of obeying Him. Briefly, God and His will, so far as we know it, must be the only right end of self-sacrifice.

Then, what is its beginning?—the passion from which it takes its rise? Usually, nay, universally, that passion which is the heart of the universe—love. The root of all true self-sacrifice is some strong affection, which makes the welfare of the beloved of more importance

to us than our own, or an equally strong devotion to a principle, which is merely an abstract
form of the same emotion.   Both these motives
are noble—and ignoble likewise, sometimes; for
the latter is often alloyed by ambition, egotism,
obstinacy, love of power; while the former is
seldom free from that recondite but very
common selfishness, the hope of having our
self-sacrifice duly appreciated.   Very few of
the most devoted of our lovers and friends
would come up to the standard I once heard
given of true affection : " He might die for you,
but he would never let you know it."

Now most of your self-sacrificers take abundant pains to let you know it.   When they
offer themselves up, it is with a lurking hope
that not only the object of so much devotion,
but a select circle of sympathizing admirers,
may be present at their immolation.   The heroic
self-control which "dies and makes no sign"
is a virtue of which very few are capable.
As I once heard commented by a small but
sage commentator on the poem of "Enoch
Arden," "Yes, it was very good of Enoch

not to tell his story until he died, but, mama, what a pity he didn't die and say nothing at all!"

There is another view of martyrdom which deserves a word. It may be a very grand thing, despite its pains, for the martyr, who has made his choice, accepted his fate, and is prepared to go up in a cloud of glory to heaven ; not unconscious, perhaps, of the eyes that will be following him thither. But what of those who have permitted or exacted the sacrifice ? And suppose it has been offered foolishly, needlessly ; perhaps even in some bitter outburst of feeling not quite so holy as the act appears ? Before we lay ourselves down before Juggernaut, is it not as well to see if he is a god, or only an ugly idol ? And in preparing our suttee, should we not pause to consider how far we are really benefiting the affectionate friends who come to assist thereat ? Possibly the rôle of victim which we are so anxious to play may affix upon some one else the corresponding title of murderer.

He who causes his brother to err is himself a

sinner. Now do you see what I mean by the *sin* of self-sacrifice?

A sin to which I fear women are much more prone than men. It is apparently a law of the universe that the male animal should be always more or less a selfish animal. No doubt there is some reason in this, some good reason; indeed we can almost trace that. A large ego is oftentimes necessary to enable a man to hold his own in the hard battle of life; and the creed of "self-preservation is the first law of nature," which presents itself so forcibly to the mind of the ordinary man, in all phases of society, from the savage to the sybarite, may contribute a good deal to the advantage of the species. Be that as it may be, I am afraid it must be owned that, with some noble exceptions, men are, as a rule, ignobly and incurably selfish. But it remains to be proved how far they are so in themselves, or how far it is the women's fault, who, by this exaggeration of unselfishness, this sinful self-sacrifice, help to make them what they are.

Despite all the fancies of lovers and poets,

throughout life, women are the offerers, and men the accepters, of an amount of devotion which would ruin an angel. They are the slaves who manufacture the tyrants.

Yet how sweet and charming it is to be a slave—at first. To a loving-hearted woman for love's sake, to a weak one because it saves trouble, lightens responsibility, and flatters that self-conscious vanity which, if we tear off its saintly robes, underlies so much devotion, amatory as well as religious, female devotion especially.

> "He for God only—she for God in him."

So wrote Milton, and few men ever wrote a more false or dangerous line. Why,—though it may be less flattering to the man, less easy for the woman,—why should not she as well as he live "for God only"? Why, instead of seeing no medium between blind idolatry or childish subserviency, and a frantic struggle after impossible "rights," should she not accept calmly her plain duty, to be man's help-meet, and assist him in doing *his* duty, before the world and before God?

Instead, how many, knowingly or unknowingly, do their very utmost not to amend but to destroy the objects of their love? For women will love men, and all the philosophers in petticoats, or less graceful habiliments, who aim at remodelling society, free from the old-fashioned folly of wifehood and motherhood, will never succeed in conquering this amiable weakness. It is all very well to pretend that women are the adored and men the adorers; so they are, for a year or two, and towards one or two women— but at the beginning and end of life, and all through it, save during the brief courtship-time, it is the business of their womenkind—mothers, sisters, wives, daughters—to worship *them*, to serve *them*, to obey *them*. Every man in his secret heart recognises this fact, and is complacently satisfied that it should remain a fact, for ever.

Well, let it be so! Perhaps the "Whole Duty of Woman" *is* man; but it is in order that she may be the agent for making him into a real man, fulfilling all the noble aims of manhood.

Gay, in his "Acis and Galatea," has one fine

line—finer, perhaps, than he meant it to be.
The nymph, changing her dead shepherd into
a fountain, says,

" Be thou immortal, since thou art not mine."

And any woman who ever truly loved a man
would desire to make him so—not "hers,"
perhaps, but "immortal;" that is, what he
ought to be, in himself, and towards God and
man. If, instead, she thinks only of what he
is to her, and what she wishes to be to him,
her love will prove, despite all its passionate
or affectionate disguises, not his blessing, but
his life-long curse.

This, though she may have shown towards
him any amount of self-sacrifice and blind devotion. If women's devotedness to men in
any relation of life teaches the latter to be
selfish, lazy, exacting, imperious, the act is
not a merit but a sin, and causes their beloved
ones to sin. In the cant phrase, which while
I use I detest, they are "setting the creature
above the Creator," and will surely reap—and
deserve—their punishment. Not, as some theo-

logians put it, in the divine revenge of a jealous God, angry that any poor mortal is loved beyond Himself—but as the inevitable result of that perfect law: "The soul that sinneth it shall die." It must; for in all sin is the seed of death, and God Himself, unless by changing His all-righteous essence, could not make it otherwise.

Therefore, if a mother by overweening indulgence helps her son to become a thoughtless scapegrace; if a wife by cowardly subserviency converts her husband into a selfish brute; even if a daughter—as in a late case of somewhat notable literary biography—sets up a weak, luxurious, unprincipled father as the idol of her life, and expects everybody to bow down and worship him;—all these foolish women have condoned sin, and called vice virtue; have left the truth and believed, or pretended to believe, a lie. When their false god falls, or turns into an avenging demon, then they come to understand what means the sin of self-sacrifice.

Sinful, in one sense, because it is often only

a disguised form of a rather ugly quality—self-will.

I heard the other day enthusiastic praises of a sister in one of those Protestant communities who are trying—and not unwisely—to emulate the Roman Catholic sisters of mercy, by absorbing into useful work the many waifs and strays of useless spinsterhood, eating their hearts out in lonely, aimless idleness in the midst of a struggling and suffering world. But this woman was not lonely. She had a father, whom she paid a nurse to take care of; married sisters, who would have been thankful for her occasional help in their busy, anxious homes; loving friends, to whom her influence and aid might often have been invaluable. Yet she left them, one and all, and went to spend her strength — not so very great—upon strangers. She did expend it; for she died, and was almost canonised by some people; but some others, with a simpler standard of holiness, might question whether this devoted self-sacrifice should not be called by another name—self-will. She did the thing she wished to do, rather than what seemed laid before her to do; and, though it is always difficult to judge such cases from the outside without being unjust to somebody, I think it is an open question whether she did right or wrong.

The same doubt arises when one hears of soldiers, volunteering—not sent, but volunteering—on dangerous expeditions, leaving young wives or helpless children to endure at home the agony of suspense over a risk which was not demanded by duty;—of missionaries, quitting the unobtrusive, useful work of a parish priest in trying to win poor Hodge from his drink, or Black Jem from his poaching, for the more exciting duty of converting a handful of savages, at a cost of about three hundred pounds per head, and at last making them not so very much better Christians than either Hodge or Jem, if these only had an equal chance of spiritual instruction.

Lastly, I own that I have no ardent admiration for those religious devotees of any sort— High Church, Low Church, or no church at all—

who, obeying an often imaginary call, "Come out from among them, and be ye separate," think that it is "the will of the Lord" they should break the hearts of parents, alienate fond friends, renounce the plain duties of daily life—and all for what? To "save their soul," as they term it! As if the saving of their own petty individual soul—whatever that phrase may mean—was a good worth the cost of so much actual evil, and to so many other souls!

Understand me. I do not deny that there is such a thing as conversion—nay, *sudden* conversion; that even in this noisy nineteenth century, as once on the silent shores of Galilee, a man may hear the voice, "Follow Me," and, leaving all, may follow Him, to wearing life-long work in East-end parishes, or in scarcely less barbarous foreign lands. But let him be quite sure first who it is that calleth him, and let him take care that the sacrifice offered is really to God, and not to his own restless, excitable, unsatisfied imagination; that, in short, it is not a sacrifice to self, rather than a self-sacrifice.

For such, alas! are a great many of the
immolations I am dealing with; especially
among women. Women, who are so strong
in their capabilities of loving, are above all
liable to that guiltiness in the form of loving,
which does incalculable harm to its object.
That is a short-sighted affection, indeed, which
causes us to help another to do wrong instead
of right. When our unselfishness makes others
selfish;—when we submit to their injustice,
condone their offences, call their errors follies,
and their follies pretty " lovablenesses;"—then
we love them in a mean, unworthy way; we
are not devotees, but idolaters.

There are women—sisters and wives—tied
to men so unworthy of the bond, that their
only safe course is, not obedience, but a little
righteous rebellion. There are men, beginning
life as very good men, who are seen slowly
growing into the bores, the torments, the
laughing-stocks of their more clear-sighted
friends; eaten up with vanity, intolerable
through self-assertion, just because their
womenkind love them—not rationally, but ir-

rationally; put them on a pedestal and worship them, expecting everybody else to do the same. But everybody does not, and so this self-devotion only makes its object ridiculous, if not contemptible, except to the poor enthusiasts, who go on adoring him still, half from habit, half from fear.

For fear is the root of many a so-called self-sacrifice. Weak natures find it so much easier to submit to a wrong than to fight against it. Less trouble also. Many lazy women prefer getting their own way in an underhand, round-about fashion, by humouring the weaknesses of the men they belong to, instead of honourably and openly resisting them, when resistance becomes necessary. That is, using the right—the only honest "right" a woman has, of asserting her independent existence before God and men, as a responsible human being, who will neither be forced to do wrong herself, nor see another do wrong, if she can help it.

Yet how many women not only err themselves, but aid and abet error, knowing it to be such, under the compulsion of that weak fear of man, which is called or miscalled "conjugal obedience."

Here—I can almost see my readers shudder —"What! not obey one's husband? What! counsel rebellion in our wives?"

Stop a moment. I never said so. On the contrary, I say distinctly, Wives, obey your husbands, as children your parents—"in the Lord." But only "in the Lord." Yield as much as possible in ordinary things; conquer your tempers, modify your tastes; give up everything, in short, that is not a compromise of principle. When it comes to that, resist! Whatever they may be to you, and how great soever your love for them, resist them. Never allow either father, husband, brother, son, to stand between you and the clear law of right and wrong in your own soul, which the God who made you has put there. If you do, you fall into that sin of which I speak, and will assuredly, soon or late, earn its bitter wages.

For how sad it is to see wives, whose husbands are inclined to extravagance, deny themselves not only lawful luxuries, but needful comforts,

in order to make up silently for the wilful waste
against which they had not the courage to protest; when, perhaps, a few words, tender as
true, would have brought the man to his right
senses, and prevented his friends from calling
him, as of course they do (behind his back), a
selfish, pleasure-loving brute. And why should
other men, crotchety, worrying, or bad-tempered,
though not really bad fellows at heart, slowly
become the torment of a whole household, because the mistress considers it her bounden
duty to force everybody into yielding to what
she euphuistically terms "papa's little ways"?
Can she not see that she is thereby destroying
all domestic comfort, and teaching both servants
and children to avoid, to fear, nay, actually to
dislike, one whom they ought to honour and love?
A grain of moral courage on her part, an honest
appeal to that generosity which lies hid in most
men's hearts, would have helped the wife to
help her husband, and, by teaching him to
restrain himself, make him a far better and
happier man than if he had been tamely yielded
to, and so converted into a sort of family ogre,

which, little as they suspect it, a good many men really are in private life.

And I think the ogre's wife in Hop-o'-my-Thumb is a very good illustration of your meek, self-sacrificing, self-devoted wives—who after all sometimes end in assisting themselves, as she did, to become happy widows. Meantime, they "do their duty" most obediently; will even help in the fattening of children for their lord's provender—other people's children, certainly. But there are women who consider it a point of duty to immolate their own.

How many stories one could record in which a wife, fancying herself a pattern of conjugal obedience, has sacrificed her children just as much as Chaucer's "Griseldis"—detestable heroine!—sacrificed hers; allowing her whole family to be worried, bullied, and otherwise evil-entreated by him whom the law presumes to be its guardian and head.

A misery—which ends not even there. For in such households brothers soon learn to treat sisters as papa treats mamma, with rough words, ceaseless grumblings, selfish exactingnesses.

Daughters, brought up to hush their voices
or run away whenever the father's step is heard
—papa, who generally comes home cross, and
requires to be coaxed and "soothed" by mamma
whenever she wants anything—these girls, accustomed to be considered inferior animals, who
must get their own way by stratagem, grow up
into those designing young ladies, who owe
their power over men to first flattering and then
deceiving them.

But what a future for the new generation!
How many unhappy girls have paid dearly for
the early upbringing of their young husbands,
who, the first glamour of love passed, treat their
wives as they were allowed to treat their sisters,
and as they saw their fathers treat their mothers,
carelessly, disrespectfully, with a total want of
that considerate tenderness which is worth all
the passionate love in the world. This—though
they may pass muster outside as excellent
husbands, never doing anything really bad, and
possessing many good and attractive qualities,
yet contriving somehow quietly to break the
poor womanly heart, or harden it into that

passive acceptance of pain, which is more fatal to married happiness than even temporary estrangement. Anger itself is a safer thing than stolid, hopeless indifference.

The best husbands I ever met came out of a family where the mother, a most heroic and self-denying woman, laid down the absolute law, "Girls first." Not in any authority; but first to be thought of, as to protection and tenderness. Consequently, the chivalrous care which these lads were taught to show to their own sisters naturally extended itself to all women. They grew up true gentlemen—gentle men—generous, unexacting, courteous of speech and kind of heart. In them was the protecting strength of manhood, which scorns to use its strength except for protection; the proud honesty of manhood, which infinitely prefers being lovingly and openly resisted, to being "twisted round one's finger," as mean men are twisted, and mean women will always be found ready to do it; but which, I think, all honest men and brave women would not merely dislike, but utterly despise.

It seems, hitherto, as if of this sin of self-sacrifice women were oftenest guilty. Not always.

I have spoken of tyranny; there is nothing so absolute as the tyranny of weakness. Sometimes a really good man will suffer himself to be so victimized by a nervous, silly, selfish wife, that he dare not call his soul his own. By a thousand underhand ways, she succeeds in alienating him from his own family—breaking his natural ties, hindering his most sacred duties; putting a stop to his honest work in the world—his rightful influence therein, and all the pleasures that belong thereto. And these being, to a man, so much wider than any woman's, the loss is the greater, the pain the sharper.

One can imagine a large-minded, honourably ambitious man actually writhing under the sacrifices forced from him by a wife, feeble in every way—who destroys not merely his happiness, but his good reputation. Since, when it is seen that her merest whims are held by him of paramount importance—that her silly, selfish Yes or No is to decide every action of his life, do not his friends laugh at him behind his back, even though before his face they may keep up a decorous gravity? "Poor fellow! with such a goose for his wife!" Yet the pity is akin to contempt; and something more than contempt is felt—especially by his mother, sisters, or critical female friends—towards that wife, who exacts from him the renunciation of all his duties, except those towards herself; in plain English, "makes a fool of him," because in his devotion he has offered everything to her, and she has meanly accepted the sacrifice.

He ought never to have made it. He ought to have given her care, tenderness, affection—all that man should give to woman, and strength to weakness; but there it should have ended. No wife has a right to claim the husband's whole life, its honourable toil, its lawful enjoyments. If she cannot share, she should learn at least not to stand in the way of either. And the man who submits to be so tyrannized over—as weak women in their small way can tyrannize, with that "continual dropping that weareth away the ·stone"—deserves all he gets; his friends' covert smiles, his enemies' unconcealed sneer.

We talk a great deal about the error of "spoiling" our children; may we not "spoil" our wives, our husbands, not to speak of other less important ties, quite as much, and as sinfully? For life is a long course of mutual education, which ends but with the grave. If we are wise enough to recognise this, and act upon it, nor be afraid of that accidental attrition which only rubs off inevitable angles—if, in short, our aim in all the dear bonds of existence is not so much to please either ourselves or one another, but to do right—which means pleasing God—then all is well. But if we shirk the right, and accept the agreeable—if we expect life to be all holidays and no school, then we shall soon begin to find out its utter weariness and worthlessness, to blame the faithless, ungrateful world—as if good done with the expectation of gratitude were ever worth anything! And we shall come to the end of it all with a dreary sense of having renounced everything and gained nothing, except, perhaps, the poor consolation of considering ourselves martyrs.

And why? Because we mistook the boundary where virtue passes into vice—self-devotion into blind and foolish, nay, sinful self-sacrifice.

There is a point beyond which we have no right to ignore our own individuality—that is, supposing we have any. Many people have none. They get the credit of being extremely self-denying, because they really have no particular self to deny. Their feeble nature is only capable of imitating others; and their stagnant placidity is no absolute virtue, but the mere negation of a vice. Even as there are many most "respectable" people, whom nothing keeps from being villains, except one fortunate fact—that they are such arrant cowards.

But to those born with decided tastes, feelings, possibly talents, the exercise of all these is an actual necessity. And lawfully so. If God has given us our little light, what right have we to hide it under a bushel, because some affectionate, purblind friend dislikes the glare of it, or fears it will set the house on fire? No; let us put it in its proper place, a safe candlestick, if it be a light, but let nobody persuade or force us to put it out.

What bitter sacrifices one member of a family gifted with a strong proclivity, perhaps even a genius, for art, music, or literature, sometimes has to make to the rest, who cannot understand it!

Now, a one-sided enthusiast—a Bernard Pallissy for instance—makes a very disagreeable husband and a still worse father of a family; and a modern Corinne, with her hair down her back, sitting playing the harp all day long, instead of going into her kitchen, ordering her dinner, and looking after her servants, would be a most aggravating wife for any man to marry. But, on the other hand, a gentleman with no ear for music, married to a wife who is a born musician, may make a very great victim of that poor lady. And the pretty commonplace girl, whom a clever man of poetical nature has idealized into an angel in the house, sometimes succeeds in slowly but completely extinguishing in him that higher life of heart and intellect—the spiritual life, compared to which the worldly life is mere dust and ashes, and even the domestic life, sweet as it is, a body without a soul.

We ought always to be chary in allowing ourselves to be forced into sacrifices which do not benefit, but merely gratify the persons exacting them. First, because a person who can be gratified by a self-sacrifice is—rather a mean person ; secondly, because to renounce any innocent taste or pursuit is not merely foolish, but wrong. All our talents were given us to use ; not to bury in a napkin. If we do so bury them, to please even the dearest friend on earth, we are guilty of not merely cowardice, but infidelity to our trust ; and depend upon it, the sacrifice will do no good to that other person and great harm to ourselves. To say nothing of the sneering comments of outsiders, and the just condemnation of wiser folk, to which we expose—not ourselves, we are exalted into martyrs—but those we love, if we love them so foolishly as to suffer them to victimize us unnecessarily.

And very sad to see is the extent to which some people are victimized in domestic life ; from bad health—bad temper, acting and reacting

upon each other, and both equally blamable ;
for miserable as the sufferers are, the cause of
their sufferings is often nobody but themselves.
To maintain a sound mind in a sound body, so as
to be a help instead of a burthen, not to say a
nuisance, to our family and friends, requires an
amount of self-control of which not everybody is
capable. Some people consider it "silly" to
be careful of health, and others find it so "interesting" to be ill—that the amount of pain,
worry, and anxiety which is inflicted by those
who allow themselves to fall into absolutely
preventible illness is very great. Equally
great is the self-sacrifice entailed upon kindly
people, who cannot stand by and see others
suffer, although deservedly, without coming to
the rescue with every help they can bring.

How often, too, do we see in a family, not
otherwise unamiable, one especial "root of bitterness," a thoroughly ill-conditioned person,
of whom all the rest stand in dread, to whom
they give up everything, and for whom they
will do anything, just for the sake of peace.
Long habit has perhaps half accustomed them

to the torment; they have learned to walk
pretty steadily under it, like a man with a
nail in his shoe—but what a torment it is! A
person who takes everything amiss, whose mood
you never can be sure of for a single hour, whom
you are obliged to propitiate, as the savages
their idols; one whom you must be on your
guard with, and make perpetual apologies for,
lest the world outside should surmise anything
wrong—with whom you never can find any rest,
and though he or she may be your nearest and
dearest, ostensibly, you are painfully conscious
that the only relief is to get away from him, or to
get him away.

I have grave doubts whether in a case of this
kind—and we all know many such, though we
are too polite to say so—it is not the duty of a
conscientious head of a family, or its members,
to take very strong measures. There are some
people so intolerable to live with that nobody
should be allowed to live with them. Every
effort should be made by the family which un-
happily owns them, to free itself from them, in
any lawful way, and at any cost of money or

inconvenience. Some who are an absolute tor-
ture to their own relations, do well enough with
strangers; the self-restraint they then are obliged to exercise is a wholesome discipline for
them, and the people they afflict, being farther
off, are not so deeply afflicted as their own kith
and kin.

Would it not be worth while, if, instead of
lauding to the skies the self-sacrifice of a family
in thus victimizing itself, we were to institute
an Asylum for Family Nuisances, to which could
be removed the cross-grained brother or sister,
the cantankerous aunt, the "difficult" relative
of any sort, whom, if not a relative, the other
members of the household would fly from as
from something harmful and hateful? Instead,
they go on enduring and enduring, till the harm
becomes irremediable. Which is the worst, to
put a detestable thing or person so far from you
that you cease to feel anything towards him save
a mild indifference? or to suffer yourself and
others to be so tormented by him, that the
sanctimonious "if it would please God to
take him "—which is only an elegant form

of murder — ceases to appear wrong, only natural ?

Yet this is what your vaunted self-sacrifice leads to, when perpetrated for the sake of unworthy people.

But there are people, amiable, interesting, affectionate (externally), to whom one sometimes sees whole families sacrificing themselves, without the slightest sense of the harm they are doing,—I mean the "ne'er-do-weels." Not the people who do actual evil, but the people who never do good. Of such is the weak, amiable, impecunious brother who always comes back and back, to drain the last halfpenny from his hard-working sisters. Perhaps he has no vices whatever, is of a pleasant and not unaffectionate nature, only somehow he contrives to let everything slip through his fingers—money, time, opportunity. And as he in reality thinks of nobody but himself, of course he marries early and rashly, and brings his wife and family to be kept by his sisters, who go on impoverishing themselves year by year, doing not only their duty—all sisters must

D

do that—but a great deal more than their duty ; submitting to endless exactions, allowing not only the feeble, who are a natural burden, but the strong, the self-indulgent, the extravagant, to live upon them, and drain the life-blood out of them, till death comes in mercy to end the never-ceasing sacrifice. A sacrifice which has done no good to anybody; for it has left the selfish selfish still, and the extravagant as reckless as ever; perhaps worse than ever, from the long habit of receiving supplies from others, instead of earning their luxuries, if they must have them, for themselves. The life-long devotion of a whole family to one unworthy member has been no more than pouring water into a sieve; it has never benefited him, and it has ruined the rest.

Another, though rarer case, and less patent to the world, we sometimes see, in which a number of unmarried sisters hang round a kind brother, as their natural guardian; which he is, within certain limits. But these limits the amiable, helpless women do not see. He enters the flower of his age, he passes it, yet still he cannot

marry—could not possibly do it, without turning
his sisters out of doors. He shrinks from that;
shrinks, too, from offering such an encumbered
hand and heart to any girl. And besides, it is
not every girl who in marrying likes to marry
a whole family. So time slips on; the more
high-minded and generous the man is, the more
complete is his sacrifice. Perhaps he gets
habituated to it, and almost content in it—but
it is none the less a sacrifice. He may be a
good and not unhappy old bachelor, but he
would have been much better and happier
married, and in a home of his very own. His
sisters too, if, though poor, they had ceased to
be helpless, had gone out into the world and
earned their own living, or if rich, they had
made for themselves an independent household,
how much higher and more perfect lives they
might have led!

Of course, there are exceptions to everything,
and sometimes a combination of sad destinies,
mutual disappointments, strong fraternal attachment, and great natural affinity make these
households of unmarried brothers and sisters

very peaceful and honourable substitutes for the better and completer domestic life. One has seen more than one such; which is more than a resting-place—a visible haven of refuge: not only to its inhabitants, but to all around. Yet there are others, upon which standers-by look with pity not unmixed with indignation. And the nobler, the more silent the sacrifice, the greater is the sadness of it—even though it cannot quite come under the name of sin.

Self-devotion—God forbid I should ever say a word in condemnation of that! It is the noblest thing in all this world, and the rarest—No, not rare: few family histories are without some heroic or pathetic instance thereof, continued throughout whole lives, with unflinching fortitude. And could death open the locked records of many a heart, how often would some secret be found there that would furnish a key to all the history of the finished life—some strong, one love—some eternal faithfulness,—which all the chances and changes of existence could never shake, which was the impulse of every thought, the motive of every action, the compelling force of every line of conduct. A devotion, not a passion, inasmuch as it was able to set itself entirely aside—absorb itself in the well-being of the other, whose good it sought, without reckoning any personal cost, through weal and woe, pleasure and pain, requital or non-requital. This is a sight—not to blame or weep over, but to rejoice in : for it is not blind self-sacrifice ; it is open-eyed self-devotion—blessed on both sides, both to the giver and receiver. It has sharp agonies sometimes—what deep emotion is without them ? but out of all come peace and content. It is pleasing in God's sight as lovely in man's, because there is no sin in it, no selfishness on either side ; and in its very sadness—it must of necessity be often sad—there is a sacredness beyond all mortal joy.

Of all forms of self-devotion, the one which, even when it amounts to absolute self-sacrifice, we cannot but regard with very tender and lenient eyes, is the devotion of the young to the old, of children to parents. No doubt, there is a boundary beyond which even this ought not to be permitted ; but the remedy lies on the elder side. There are such things as unworthy, selfish, exacting parents, to whom duty must be done, simply for the sake of parenthood, without regarding their personality. "Honour thy father and thy mother" is the absolute command, bounded by no proviso as to whether the parents are good or bad. Of course no one can literally "honour" that which is bad—still one can respect the abstract bond, in having patience with the individual.

But I think every high or honourable instinct in human nature will feel that there is hardly a limit to be set to the devotion of a child to a good parent—righteous devotion, repaying to failing life all that its own young life once received, of care and comfort and blessing. And no good, or even moderately good parent is ever likely to allow this devotion to pass into self-sacrifice. Surely, as long as conscious-ness and reason lasted, all true fathers and mothers would prevent, in all possible ways, the complete absorption of the younger life into theirs ; nor allow their poor expiring flame to be kept alight a few years, a few months, by the vital breath of a far more valuable existence.

But if such a case does happen—the child alone, and no outsider, has a right to decide upon the due extent of the sacrifice, and how far it is necessary or beneficial, even to the aged sufferers themselves. There may be a point beyond which the most affectionate child has no right to go— but must pause and judge whether a duty, which inevitably overrides all other duties, has not in it something amiss; even as a love which destroys all other loves, cannot fail to deteriorate the whole being.

And here, reasoning in a circle, we come round to the point from whence we started—" He that loveth father or mother "—or any other—" more than Me "—that is, he who allows his love for them to make them err against Me—"is not worthy of Me." Therefore all self-sacrifice, made solely for the love of man, or for the gratification of some merely human ambition, is not a righteous but a sinful thing—and, as sin, will assuredly find its punishment.

This furnishes, apparently, a solution to

the great mystery, why so many noble self-sacrifices are so futile, so aimless, so positively injurious? "I am the Lord thy God; thou shalt have none other Gods but me." If we make to ourselves idols, of any sort—that is, if we allow love to conquer right, and set aside what we ought to do in favour of what we like to do, we suffer accordingly—and God Himself, who is justice as well as mercy, cannot save us from suffering. And this is what I meant when I first called this sermon the Sin of Self-sacrifice.

Sermon II.

OUR OFTEN INFIRMITIES.

II.

OUR OFTEN INFIRMITIES.

DOES it ever occur to those of us who are no longer young—who begin to feel this wonderful machine a little the worse for wear, while its spiritual inmate is as fresh and strong as ever, how low apparently is the standard of health in this present generation? How seldom among our friends and acquaintances can we point out a thoroughly healthy person? I will not even say a robust person, but one who has sufficient vitality of body to keep up the daily requirements of his mental work, or any sort of work, without complaining, without having continually to resort to extraneous helps, medical or hygienic, wherewith to bolster up his failing powers, and make him capable of his necessary duties.

We do not need to reach the first half-century of life in order to see our compeers, and alas! too often others much younger in the race, drop out of it one by one—sink into miserable valetudinarians, or, growing old before their time, slip from the active enjoyment of life into the mere endurance of it. How many among us who only yesterday, as it were, seemed ready for an eternity of youth and labour—to whom threescore years and ten appeared all too short for what they had to do, now consciously or unconsciously echo the pathetic words of one whose name I this day write with tears, for Charles Kingsley only yesterday "fell on sleep : "—

"Men must work, and women must weep,
And the sooner it's over the sooner to sleep."

Nay, all have not even strength to work, and some scarcely enough strength to weep, but drop into helpless silence and a weary looking forward to that death-slumber which is to them the only possible rest. I have heard people say they do not even want to "go to heaven;" they only want to go to sleep. They are "so tired."

Why so? Why, in an age supposed to be thus civilised—over-civilised indeed; which takes such exceeding care of itself, mentally and physically; writes cartloads of medical books and makes speeches by the hour on sanitary subjects,—is the old-fashioned health of our forefathers a thing almost unknown? True, we are said to live longer than they did, but what sort of life is it? Do we enjoy the full vigour of a sound mind in a sound body, to be used both for the service of God and man; good at work, good at play; able to make the very most of every hour? Are we wholesome trees bearing fruit to the last, and still keeping "strong and well-liking"? Or do we, immediately after our first youth, often before it is ended, begin to fade and fail, to grumble at our work, to weary of our pleasures, to be pestered ourselves, and, worse, to pester all our friends, with our "often infirmities"? Not actual sicknesses, but infirmities; small sufferings of all sorts, and a general sense of incapacity for the duties of life, which entirely takes away its happy normal condition—not to think about one's self at all.

When a man makes a habit of dwelling upon his sins, depend upon it he has a good many sins to dwell on ; and he who persists in "investigating his own inside" will very soon fall, if he has not already fallen, into a thoroughly diseased state. Even as truly good people are good without knowing it, so really healthy people never notice their health. The perfect life is the child's life of absolute unconsciousness.

But this is a condition so rare nowadays, whatever it was in days past, that the question of our often infirmities, to borrow an apostolic phrase, deserves a sermon quite as much as many topics which are discussed in pulpits, where it is mostly the fashion to attend to the soul first and the body afterwards.

Not very long ago I heard a clergyman seriously proclaim that "the Gospel" must first be given to the starving, sinning, suffering denizens of London courts and alleys—the Gospel first, and food, clothes, soap and water, and decent dwellings afterwards. It is one of the trying things of going to church that whatever a man says one must hear him ; one cannot stand up and contradict him ; else I should like to have suggested to this well-meaning but narrow-visioned preacher, how much a man's moral nature depends upon his surroundings. Diogenes might not have been a cynic if he had not lived in a tub ; and I doubt if the noblest man alive, if compelled to inhabit a pigsty, would long remain much better than a swine.

Therefore it behoves us to take heed that the corporeal habitation into which our spirit is put —for this life at least—is dealt with as kindly as circumstances allow, carefully cherished, swept and garnished, and made the most commodious residence possible, so as to allow free play to its immortal inhabitant.

It is true—too true, alas !—that in many instances this desirable end is neutralised by hereditary weaknesses—the sins of the fathers inevitably visited upon the children ; and by our own early faults ignorantly committed, and the unalterable circumstances in which our lot is placed. We cannot care for ourselves without sacrificing more than ought to be sacrificed

by any hnman being to his own individuality.
But there is a medium course always possible;
and sore let and hindered as we may often be,
I think some of us very often create our own
hindrances and add weight to our natural burdens by the want of a certain respect for the
body, as a faithful servant, out of whom we must
get a good deal of work before we have done
with it.

We generally begin by working it a great
deal too hard. We rejoice in our youth; we
exult in our strength; we use both recklessly,
boastfully, as if they were wholly our own to
do as we liked with, and could never possibly
wear out. So, in a thousand careless ways, we
squander vitality, never thinking that we have
only a certain quantity given us to last till
death, and that for every atom of wasted health,
heedlessly wasted — nature, that is God, will
assuredly one day bring us to judgment.

Still, we are not wholly to blame. I believe
many feeble men or delicate women of to-day
owe the helplessness of their lives to the ignorance of sanitary laws of the parents of forty

or fifty years ago. Even as fifty years hence our children may have to reproach us for that system of over-feeding, and especially over-drinking, which many doctors now advocate for the young generation. I doubt if even the calomel powders, jalap and gin, brimstone and treacle, of our tormented childhood, were worse than the meat three times a day, the brandy and the daily glass of wine, poured into innocent little stomachs, which naturally would keep to the infant's food of bread and milk, and almost nothing besides. Certainly, not stimulants.

This is neither a medical treatise nor a tee-total essay, yet, as he is a coward who does not openly advance his colours, I do not hesitate to say that I believe half the bodily and spiritual ailments of this world spring from that much misinterpreted and not by any means inspired sentence of St. Paul, "Drink no longer water, but take a little wine for thy stomach's sake and thy often infirmities." How often do we hear it quoted. But nobody considers that the advice was given *because of* the "often infirmities," the origin of which we, of

E

course, do not know. That which is most
valuable as a medicine, is poison when taken
as a food. To accustom a child, or a youth, to
strong drinks, is to institute a craving after
them—a necessity for them—almost more dangerous than the temporary good, if it be a good,
effected by their use.

Most children have an instinctive dislike to
alcohol in any shape; unless, indeed, there be
an hereditary predisposition towards it—of all
predispositions the most fatal. Any one who
knows the strong pureness of a constitution
which has received from two or three temperate
generations an absolute indifference to stimulants, can hardly overvalue the blessing it is
to a child, boy or girl, to bring it up from
babyhood in the firm faith that wine, beer, and
spirits are only medicines, not drinks; that
when you are thirsty, be you man, woman, or
child, the right and natural beverage for you
is water, and only water. If you require it, if
you have been so corrupted by the evil influences
of your youth, or the luxurious tastes of your
after years, that you "cannot drink water,"

either there is something radically diseased in your constitution, or you will soon bring yourself to that condition. Long before you are middle-aged you will have no lack of "often infirmities."

I could write pages on the folly—the absolute madness, of parents, in allowing unlimited beer to growing lads, daily glasses of wine to over-worked, delicate girls. Nay, descending to the very root of things, I would implore all parents who wish their sons to have the strength of a Samson, to remember Manoah's wife, and suffer neither doctors nor old women to persuade them that strong drinks are essential to even a nursing mother; but that that mother is specially wise, specially blessed—ay, and her children will rise up and call her so—who has had the self-restraint and courage to make them, before their birth and after, in the solemn language of Holy Writ, "Nazarites from their mother's womb."

To "drink no wine nor strong drink," to be absolutely independent of the need for it, or the temptation to it,—any young man or woman

brought up on this principle has not only a
defence against many moral evils, but a physical
stronghold always in reserve to fall back upon,
when accidental sickness and the certain feeble-
ness of old age call for that resource, which I
do not deny is at times a most valuable one.
But the advice I would give to the young and
healthy is this : Save yourselves from all spirit-
uous drinks, as drinks, as long as ever you can ;
even as you would resist using a crutch as long
as you had your own two legs to walk upon.   If
you like wine—well, say honestly you take it because you like it, that you prefer indulging your
palate at the expense of your health ; but never
delude yourself, or suffer others to delude you,
that alcohol is a necessity, any more than stays
or orthopœdic instruments, or strong medicinal
poisons, or other sad helps which nature and
science provide to sustain us in our slow but
sure decay.

Still, to retard that decay as much as possible,
to keep up to the last limit the intellectual and
physical vigour which is such a blessing, not
only to ourselves but to those about us, this is

the religion of the body—too often lost sight of—
but which I for one count it no heathenism both
to believe in and to preach. A religion, not a
superstition; the reverence and care for the physical temple of the divine human soul, without
in the least sinking to that luxurious Greek philo-
sophy which considered the body only as worth
regarding.

On the contrary, if we must be either Syba-
rites or Spartans, better be Spartans. The
harsh and rough upbringing of our grandmothers probably did less harm than the present system of mingled over-care and carelessness. If they thought too little of children,
made them often poor miserable victims to
their elders; we, nowadays, see ourselves
victimised to the younger generation rather
too much. They also suffer; in fact, to use the
common phrase, are "killed with kindness."
Parents will not see that a child is safer turned
out to play in all weathers than shut up from
the least breath of wind in nurseries so ill
ventilated that the air is actually fetid. And
people who would shudder at the idea of their

boys and girls running about barefooted, take them (in low-necked, sleeveless muslin frocks, which leave exposed the most sensitive region, the chest and upper arm, or velvet tunics that do not reach to the shivering little knees)—take them to children's parties, where they must necessarily encounter chills, which to the young are absolute death, and eat food which to their tender stomachs is all but poison. There they stay, in a heated room or in draughty passages, sitting up till their innocent eyes are shutting with sleep, or blazing with feverish and premature excitement, till ten, eleven, and even twelve o'clock, and then are carried off to bed. Next morning the parents wonder that poor little Tommy is cross, or Mary ill, or that Lucy and Charlie cannot attend to their lessons as they ought to do. How should they? Wholesome amusement—and plenty of it—is essential at all ages; and children's society most beneficial to children; but that pitiful imitation of the "show" society now cultivated by fashionable elders, which is slowly drifting downwards to corrupt the children, ought to be resisted by

wise parents with all their might. Not merely
on moral, but on simply physical grounds. Any
person who gives or goes to ordinary "children's
parties" of this sort is, I think, guilty of a wholesale massacre of the innocents. Worse than
massacre—slow murder; for such entertainments
lay the foundations of half the infirmities of
which I write, which sap the very springs of life,
and embitter all its enjoyments.

If our parents sin against us in our childhood,
how often do we sin against ourselves in youth
—that daring youth, which thinks it will always
last, and resents the slightest interference with
its whims or its privileges? It will have what
it likes, at any cost. What an endless and
thankless task it is to represent to a young girl
the common-sense fact, that to put on her warm
jacket or waterproof cloak, a sensible hat for
her head, and a stout pair of boots for her feet,
and go cheerily out, even on the wettest or
coldest day, will do her no harm, but good—
bring the roses to her cheeks and the sunshine
to her spirit; whereas to cower over the fire in
a warm woollen dress, and then undress herself

for a ball—to dance till she is heated and exhausted, and then go and sit on the stairs or by an open window to cool herself—is more than folly, it is insanity. But you, poor mother or aunt, might talk yourself hoarse; she will not listen. The one thing she likes, the other she does not like; and therefore she does the first, and will not do the second.

Young men, also, they will go their own way; sow their wild oats—and reap them. I do not speak of extreme cases of reckless dissipation, upon which retribution follows only too swift and sure, but of small dissipations, petty sins. A young fellow will dance till four in the morning several times a week, when he knows that every day in the week he must be at his office at nine — and is, being an honest fellow who wishes to get on in the world. But he does not consider how much he takes out of himself in life, and health, and strength; and sometimes out of his master's pocket too; for, with the best intentions, he cannot possibly do his work as well as it ought to be done. But he, too, does what he likes best to do, and deludes himself that it is the best; and all the arguments in the world will never convince him to the contrary.

No more will they convince those other sinners—whose sin looks so like virtue—the clever men who kill themselves with over-study;—the ambitious men who sacrifice everything to the mad desire of getting on in the world; of being —not better, or wiser, or greater—but merely richer than their neighbours.

To do work for work's sake, moderately, levelly, rationally, so as to preserve the power of doing it for the longest term that nature allows—this, the noblest aim a man can start with, becomes often swamped in the ignoble one of working merely to be superior to somebody else. Thus many a man who has earned, or is earning, enough to live comfortably, and bring up his children well—and sufficiently well off, too, to begin with a fair start where their father did—goes on slaving and toiling, his wife aiding and abetting him, in order to maintain them in the luxury to which he has risen. A paternal devotion, which has its touching phase; and yet it is as blind as it is foolish. The children would be much better left to make their own way, and earn their own bread, like their father before them. And the father himself, by the time he has accumulated the thirty, forty, or fifty thousand which he has gradually learned to consider essential to happiness—she, sly jade! has slipped away from him. He catches her, but she is like the crushed butterfly that his boys catch under their caps; all her beauty is gone. Utterly worn out with work, he can neither enjoy life himself nor give enjoyment to other people. The strain of occupation gone, his weariness becomes intolerable. The irritability that an overtasked body and mind superinduces in most men, makes him, not a delight, but an actual nuisance in his family. Those "often infirmities" which he had once no time to think much about, now rise up like murdered ghosts to torment him wherever he goes. His handsome house, his country leisure or town pleasure, his abundance of friends, and his flourishing family, are to him no comfort, no resource. He has burnt the candle at both ends, and now there is no light left in it; it just flickers awhile, and then—drops out.

I ask earnestly, Is this picture overdrawn? Do I not paint the likeness—not of one, but of hundreds—of rich men among our acquaintance in this " golden age "? Midas himself could not have more bitterly applied the word. The old king of fable, whose touch turned everything to gold, was not more wretched than some of our would-be millionaires.

For what is the use of money? Simply, to be used; to gain a certain amount of bodily comfort, for which the poor failing body is, as it gets older, only too thankful; and an equal share of intellectual pleasures and tastes, which money only can fully supply. Beyond that no man can spend, or ought to spend, upon himself. And even this, carefully employed, will always leave a large margin for the keenest pleasure of all—the money that is spent upon other people.

Idleness may be a great folly, but overwork, to no nobler end than to get rich, is a great

crime. And the men who commit it, and the
women who encourage them in it, deserve all
they get, in the secret miseries that underlie all
their splendours. What these are they know.
The indigestions of their dinner-parties, the
weariness of their balls, the worry of their
servants, the rivalries of their neighbours.
Who that looks at them as sitting, pallid and
cross, in their grand carriages, or watches the
discontent into which their bland dinner-table
face falls the moment the smile is off it, or
notices the scarcely veiled relief of the polite
adieu with which such an entertainment is
ended—"and a good thing it's over," say both
host and guest in their secret hearts—who that
takes quiet heed of all this can help feeling that
such magnificence has cost very dear? *Le jeu,
ne vaut pas la chandelle.* The paradise may be
fair enough outside, but "the trail of the
serpent is over it all."

This, without any complaints about "this
poor dying world," or the wickedness of the
people that are in it. It is a good world, a
happy world. God meant it to be happy. It

is man only who makes it miserable. For one half—perhaps nearly the whole—of these often infirmities which torment us so, Nature is not accountable; Nature, always a wise and tender mother to those who follow her dictates in the simplest way. For instance, who will deny that a number of those illnesses which we suffer from year by year are absolutely preventible illnesses?

The common answer to that commonest of moans, "I have such a bad cold,"—"Dear me! How did you catch it?"—often makes us cross enough. As if it could be any consolation in our sufferings to investigate how we got them! But the remark is not so ridiculous as it seems. It would be a curious and useful register of personal statistics, if we were to count how many of our illnesses we bring on ourselves by neglect of those common sanitary laws, which can never be broken with impunity. Men of science, half of whom allege that nature is all benign, the other half that she is wholly cruel, seem to be both right and both wrong. She is neither kind nor cruel; she is only just. She

—or a higher Power through her—lays down laws, which, so far as we see, are laws for the general good; they must be obeyed, and by all, or all suffer; and neither God nor nature can prevent this suffering.

Thus, some illnesses are not preventible. They come to us apparently " by the visitation of God," from no cause at all; that is, from recondite causes, too remote for us either to detect or guard against, but no doubt also the result of broken laws. We can but try to discover these laws, so as to obey them better another time. But a large number of our lesser ailments are entirely our own fault. We can trace in them cause and effect, as plainly as that two and two make four. That severe bronchitis which attacked us, because in the brilliant March sunshine, and fierce east wind, we put off our slightly shabby winter jacket in favour of more spring-like attire. That horrible sick headache, which we know as well as possible will follow after eating certain foods or drinking certain wines, yet we can no more resist either, than our infant boy can resist clutching at the lighted candle, or our drunken cabman at the gin-bottle. We call the child an "ignorant baby," the drunkard "a fool;" yet in what are we better than they? For the sake of petty vanity, or still more petty table-indulgence, we have punished ourselves, and tormented our whole family. The sickness which comes direct from heaven deserves all sympathy and tenderness : that brought on by a mere folly, or weak self-indulgence, though it is obliged to be nursed and cared for, is done so with a compassion bordering on contempt.

Yes, even though we call our errors by grand names, and almost boast of them, "I never take care of myself;" "I can't be bothered with my health;" "What does it matter to me if I am ill?" are the remarks one constantly hears, especially from the young, just old enough to shirk authority and resent interference, but still seeing only in the dim distance that dark time which must come, sooner or later, when for every ill-usage it has received, the body avenges itself tenfold.

Does it not matter indeed?—the extra labour

thrown on a whole family when one member is ill? the heart-ache of parents, the perplexity and distress of friends, the serious annoyance—to put no stronger word—that invalids always are in a household? If, as to our would-be suicides, the law of the land, even when it saves them from the river half drowned, or cuts them down half hanged, sentences them to remorseless punishment, should there not be found also some fitting condemnation for those who commit the slow suicide of ruined health, for no cause but their own gratification?

One of the worst forms of these is so countenanced by society that he is a bold man who would lift his voice against it; I mean the present system of dinner-parties. And yet there can be no doubt that, if it does not kill wholesale, it injures the average constitutions of what we call the "better classes," and causes them dyspeptic and other torments to an extent worse perhaps than even the hunger, or the half-feeding, which the poor have to fight against. Nobody likes to be called a glutton or a gourmand, yet the ordinary dinner-giver or diner-out of the present day will find considerable difficulty in preventing himself from becoming a little of both.

Now, a good dinner is an excellent thing. A really elegant dinner, well cooked, well served, with tasteful accompaniments of every kind, and with a moderate number of pleasant people to enjoy it, is a most delightful thing. It is right that those who can afford it should give such, replete with "every delicacy of the season;" the best food, the best wine, the most artistic and beautiful table arrangements, and in sufficient quantity fully to satisfy the guests. Sufficient time also should be allowed fairly to enjoy the meal; taking it leisurely, and seasoning it with that cheerful conversation which is said to help digestion. In truth, there cannot be a pleasanter sight than an honest, honourable man, at the head of his own hospitable board, looking down two lines of happy-looking friends, whom he is sincerely glad to welcome, and who are glad in return to give him, according to the stereotyped phrase, "the pleasure of their company," which really

F

is a pleasure, and without which the grandest
banquets are weariness inexpressible. But the
dinner should be subservient to the guests,
not the guests to the dinner; and every meal,
be it simple or splendid, is worthless altogether
unless eaten, as a good Christian has it, "in
gladness and singleness of heart." Such a meal,
taken among friends and neighbours, with the
faces of those you love, or like, or even only
admire, gathered round you, not too many of
them, nor for too long a time, and moving early
into the drawing-room, to pass a social evening
in conversation or music,—such a feast is truly a
feast; the ideal dinner-party, which does no harm
to any one, and to many a great deal of good.

But the ordinary "dinner-party " is, eighteen
or twenty people chosen at random without
any regard to their suiting one another, sitting
down to eat and drink without intermission
for from two to three hours, say from half-past
seven or eight till nearly ten. A "feed" lasting
so long that however small may be the bits
you put into the unhappy stomach, it is kept
working on at the process of digestion till its

powers are thoroughly exhausted. And, eating over, drinking begins.

I beg pardon, nobody ever "drinks" nowadays. And, of course, nobody is so vulgar as to over-eat himself. That enormity is left to the workhouse boy over his Christmas plum-pudding, or the charity girl at a school tea. Nevertheless, one sometimes sees, even in elegant drawing-rooms, gentlemen enter with fishy eyes, and talk, not too brilliantly, to ladies with flushed cheeks and weary smiles. Sometimes one would like to whisper, "My dear friends, you don't know it; but have you not both eaten and drunk a little more than was good for you? You would have felt much better and happier after a simple, short dinner, which —instead of the fifteen minutes that you stand sipping your tea, and wondering if your carriage is come—left you an hour or two to spend a pleasant, sociable evening. Has it been pleasant? Have you really enjoyed yourself? How do you feel after it? And how do you think you will feel to-morrow morning?"

Ah, that to-morrow morning! especially to

those who have to work with their brains, and
in London, apart from the wholesome country
life, which neutralises so many evils. "I can't
dine out," has said to me more than one learned
or literary man, or agreeable "homme de
société," whom dinner-givers would give the
world to get. "It is absolute death to me—or
dyspepsia, which is only a slow death to all one's
faculties, and perhaps one's moral nature too,
for your dyspeptic is usually the most ill-tem-
pered and disagreeable fellow going. And
yet I am neither a glutton nor a wine-bibber.
I like a good dinner, and I like to eat it in
company with my fellow-creatures. But, according to the present system of dinner-parties, I
can't do it without absolute injury to myself;
hindering my work, affecting my health, and
bringing on all sorts of infirmities, that a man
likes to steer clear of as long as he can."

Yes, if he has the strength of will to do it.
But not every man has, or woman either. Few
people practise that golden rule of health, I
think it was Luigi Cornaro's, "Always rise
from table feeling that you could take a little

bit more." Yet if we did practise it, with another very simple rule, to eat always regularly, at the same hour, and, as nearly as possible, the same quantity of food—not doubling the quantity because it happens to be " nice,"—we should soon lessen amazingly our often infirmities.

Prevention is better than cure, and in most small ailments there cannot be a safer physic than abstinence. Abstinence from over-food, over-work. How persistently we shut our eyes to the beginnings of disease, beginnings so trifling that we hardly notice them, until they end in that premature decay which seems now only too common amongst our best and greatest men, and those whom the world can least spare. People rush to doctors to cure them ; they never think of curing themselves, by putting a stop to the exciting causes of ill-health. As a wise old woman said to a very foolish young one, who brought her a heap of feeble MSS. to look over and try to sell, on the pitiful plea that she must have money, in order to pay for her medicine and her wine, " My dear, stop the wine and stop the medicine, and then you will be able to stop the writing also, which will be much the better for both yourself and the public."

The selfishness of people who will not stop, who go on indulging their luxurious, careless, or studious habits until they make themselves confirmed invalids, an anxiety and a torment to those about them, cannot be too strongly reprobated. Ay, even though it takes the form of a noble indifference to self, in pursuit of knowledge, wealth, ambition ; any of the pretty disguises in which we wrap up the thing we like to do, and make believe to other people, often almost to ourselves, that it is the very thing we ought to do.

And here I must dwell a moment on a case in point, the right and wrong of which is sometimes exceedingly difficult to define—how far it is allowable to run risks of infectious diseases.

Formerly, very good people regarded plague and pestilence as coming direct from the hand of God, which it was useless, nay, worse, irreligious, to fight against. I have heard sensible and excellent persons say calmly, as a reason for going, quite unnecessarily, into a fever-stricken

house, " Oh, I am not afraid : if it is the will of
the Lord for me to catch it, I shall catch it ; if
not, I am safe."

Most true ; in fact the merest truism, like
pious folks' habit of writing D.V., *Deo volente*,
about anything they intend to do, as if they
could possibly do it *without* the will of God !
But is it the will of God that infection should
be spread from house to house by these well-
meaning individuals, who may indeed escape
themselves, but can never tell how much misery
they are bringing on other people ?

Modern science has found out that, like many
other physical woes, epidemic or contagious
diseases are principally owing to ourselves, our
own errors or carelessnesses, not the will of God
at all ; that He has provided certain antidotes
or remedies against them, and those who neglect or refuse these lay themselves under the
lash of His righteous punishments, nor can they
complain of any suffering that follows.

Infectious diseases may be almost always
put under the category of preventible evils, and
it is the duty of all truly religious persons to

help the Almighty, so to speak, that is to make themselves His instruments in stamping out evil wherever they find it. Ay, even though it may be after His own mysterious way, as we sometimes see it, or fancy we do, of sacrificing the few to the many.

Disease must be stamped out, and its circle of misery narrowed as much as possible, even at cost of individual feeling. The primary thought of every person attacked by an infectious illness ought to be, "Let me harm as few people as I can." There is something particularly heroic in the story of the East-end clergyman, who, discovering that he had caught small-pox, resolutely refused to go home, would not even enter a cab which was brought to take him to the hospital, but, hailing a hearse passing by, crept into that, and so was carried safely to the safe hospital-door.

He was a noble instance, this man, of that prudence which is compatible with the utmost courage, the deepest self-devotion; that benevolent caution which sees other people's rights as clearly as its own. How different from a certain

affectionate mother, who, when another mother
hesitated to enter a railway carriage full of children because her little boy was recovering from
measles, answered, " Oh, how kind of you to tell
me! for my little folks here have only just got
through scarlet fever, and suppose they had
caught measles on the top of that?" But it
never occurred to her to prevent somebody
else's little boy from catching scarlet fever on
the top of measles.

Absolute justice, beyond even sympathy, and
far beyond sentimental feeling of any kind,
should be the rule of all who have to do with
infection; their one prominent thought how to
narrow its fatal work within the smallest possible bounds. Doctors, nurses, and those friends
and relations who are naturally in charge of
the sick, must take their lives in their hands,
do their duty, and trust God for the rest. And
happily there is seldom any lack of such; brave
physicians, who, having voluntarily entered a
profession which involves so much risk to them
and theirs, carry it out unflinchingly; nurses,
who to their own people or to strangers, for

love or for charity, which means for God, devote themselves open-eyed to a righteous self-sacrifice. But there it should end. Every one who heedlessly or unnecessarily, for bravado or thoughtlessness, or even from mistaken pious zeal, goes in the way of infection, or helps in the spread of it, commits a crime against society, which society cannot too strongly protect itself from.

When I see rabid religionists carrying handfuls of tracts into reeking, typhus-doomed cottages, where they ought first to have carried food and clothes, or, better still, have levelled them with the ground and built up in their stead wholesome dwellings; when I hear clergymen with young families, and going daily into other families and schools, protest that it is " their duty " to enter infected houses in order to administer spiritual consolation to people dying of small-pox or scarlet fever; I look upon them much as I would upon a man who thought it "his duty" to carry a lighted candle into a coal-mine. Nothing may happen; but if anything does happen, what of him who caused the disaster by his fatal folly—misnamed faith ? As if "salvation" did not mean a saving from sin rather than from punishment ; and, therefore, though men's souls may be in our hands during life, they must be left solely in God's when death comes—and after. These so-called religious persons are apparently much more bent upon doing their own will in their own way than the Master's in His way. For the will of God, so far as we can trace it through His manifestation of himself in His Son, seems to be the prevention and cure of not only moral but physical evil by every possible means, prior to its total extinction.

Either Christ's doctrine is true or it is not ; but even those who aver that it is not true often mournfully acknowledge that it ought to be—that we should be better if it were true. And He did not despise the body. He held it to be the "temple of the Holy Spirit." Asceticism was as far from Him as was luxurious living. He went about, not only teaching but doing good—practical good. Before He attempted to preach to the multitude, He fed them, remembering that " divers of them came from far." When He raised from the dead Jairus' daughter, He "commanded that something should be given her to eat." And in revisiting His forlorn disciples His first tender words were, " Children, have ye any meat ?" In no way, from beginning to end of His ministry, does He disregard or despise those bodily infirmities which we may conclude He shared, though how much or how little we never can know.

One fact, however, is noteworthy : He never complained of them. At least, the only record we have of any murmur from His lips was made solely to His Father :—" Let this cup pass from me "—followed quickly by the acceptation of it— " Not my will, but Thine be done." A lesson to us, who are so prone to grumble over the most trifling of our infirmities, the least of our aches and pains ; so ready to blame everybody for them, except ourselves ; to rush for cure to every doctor we hear of, instead of trusting to our own common-sense, self-restraint, and, when all else fails, that quiet patience which at least never inflicts its own sufferings upon its neighbours.

Christ did not—not to the very end. When dying the most torturing of deaths, it was His mother and His brethren that He thought of, not Himself. And so it is with many a sick and dying person, who in life has been a humble follower of Him.

Strange, how in these sermons, professedly " out of Church "—holding up the banner of no set creed—appealing especially to those who say they believe none, and refuse to accept any foregone conclusions, or take anything granted in the " science of theology " so called—as if any finite being could learn the Infinite as he learns astronomy or mathematics !—it is strange, I say, how continually I find myself recurring to Christ and His teaching, which—whatever be the facts or misrepresentations of His personal history— shines out clearly after the mists of ' nearly nineteen hundred years as the only perfect righteousness the world ever saw ; a standard which, consciously or unconsciously, all righteous souls instinctively recognise.

It is easy for people to say they do not believe in Christianity—that is, in its corruptions ; but the spirit of it has so permeated our modern world that many a fierce sceptic is a good Christian without knowing it. He can deny, but he cannot get away from, the influence of that divine morality which Christians recognise as their Sun of Righteousness. It may not shine ; mists may obscure it, so that one is prone to doubt its very existence ; but, without it, daylight would not be there.

I am wandering a little from my subject, and yet not far ; since what comfort is there, except in such thoughts as these, when the dark time comes which must come to us all—when our infirmities are not "often," but continual ? How shall we bear them ? How shall we meet that heavy season, when—as, I lately heard one lady answer to another who was saying she felt better than she had done for years—"Ah, my dear, but *I* shall never feel better any more " ?

Not very wonderful, considering the sufferer was seventy-six ; yet she evidently felt it a great hardship, a cruel wrong. Even then she could not reconcile herself to old age, to the gradual slipping off of the worn garment, meant tenderly, I think, as nature's preparation for the putting of it off altogether, and being clothed afresh with something, we know not what, except that it will be altogether new.

A hard time this to many; when all the sins they ever committed against their bodies—and you may sin against your body just as fatally as you sin against your soul—rise up in judgment against them. The season, when we begin to feel that we are really growing old, and that everybody sees it, but is too polite to say so, or tries to gloss it under the unmeaning remark, "How young you look!"—indicating that we cannot reasonably be expected to look young any longer. This is as painful a phase as any our life goes through—more painful, I think, than absolute old age, which gradually becomes as conceited over its many years as youth is over its few ones.

Still, I cannot believe but that it is possible, by extra care at the beginning of decay, to avoid its saddest infirmities, and to make senility a comparatively painless thing—free from many of those weaknesses and unpleasantnesses which cause so many unselfish people to say honestly they never wish to live to be old.

For instance, how few recognise the very simple and obvious truth, that as the machinery of digestion begins to wear out, it is advisable to give it some little less work to do. A meal from which a young man would rise up hungry, is quite sufficient for the needs of a man of seventy, and better for him than more. The healthiest, most active, and most happy-minded of old people I have always found to be those who were exceedingly moderate in their food ; eating less and less every year, instead of, according to the common fallacy, more and more. And they who have longest retained their hold on life and its enjoyments, have been those who in all their habits have gradually gone back to the simplicity of childhood. Indeed, it seems as if nature, when we do not foolishly resist her or interfere with her, would fain bring us back quietly to all the tastes, pleasures, and wants of our earliest youth—its innocent interests, its entire but not necessarily painful or humiliating dependence ; would give us, in short, a little tender rock in our second cradle before she lays us in the grave.

And this, if we could only see it, is good for us, and equally good for those that have to do it for us. It is well for the younger generation to see how contentedly we can loose our hold upon that world which is slowly sliding from us. Though, unlike them, we can no longer work all day and dance all night; though we require every year more care, more regularity of hours and meals, more sleep—at all events more rest; can by no means play tricks with ourselves, for any excuse either of amusement or labour; are perhaps obliged to spend one half the day in peaceful seclusion, or equally peaceful endurance of pain, in order to qualify ourselves for being cheerful with those we love for the other half;—still life is not yet a burden to us, and we try to be as little of a burden as possible to those about us. We have had our day; we will not grudge them theirs.

I cannot imagine an old age like this to be a sad or undesirable thing. Infirmities it may have—must have; but they need not be over-

G

whelming; if the failing body has been treated, and is still treated, with that amount of respect which is its due. And at worst, perhaps bodily sufferings are not harder to bear than the horrible mental struggles of youth, with its selfish agony of passion and pain; or than the vicarious sufferings of middle age, when we groaned under the weight of other people's cares, mourned over sorrows that we were utterly powerless to cure, and looked forward with endless anxiety into an uncertain future, not considering how soon it would become the harmless past.

Now all that is over. The old never grieve much; at least, not over much. Why should they? It is strange to notice how, even after a loss by death that a few years before would have utterly crushed them, they seem to rise up and go on their way—only a few steps more—quietly, even cheerfully; troubling no one, complaining to no one, probably because it is only a few steps more. Suffering itself grows calm in the near view of rest.

Thus it is with people of restful and patient mind. For others there is still something left. " I have had all I wanted," said to me one of the most unquiet spirits I ever knew, keenly alive still, even under the deadness of seventy odd years. "Life has been a long puzzle to me, but I am coming to the end of it now. There is one thing more : I want to find out the great secret, and I shall ; before long."

One can quite well imagine some people, to whom the after life was neither a certainty nor even a hope, looking forward to death as a matter of at least curiosity. But for us, who believe that death is the gate of life, it is quite a different feeling. Putting it on the very lowest ground, to have all our curiosity gratified, to know even as we are known, to feel nearer and nearer to our hands the key of the eternal mystery, the satisfying of the infinite desire,— this alone is consolation, in degree, for our own failing powers and flagging spirits ; nay even for the slowly emptying world around us— emptying of the wise and the good, the pleasant and the dear, whom one by one we see passing "*ad majores.*"

"If I could only get rid of my body I should

be all right," sighed once a great sufferer. And there are times when even the most patient of us feel rather glad that we do not live for ever. Respect our mortal tabernacle as we may, and treat it tenderly, as we ought to do, we may one day be not so very sorry to lay it down, not only with all its sins, but with its often infirmities.

Sermon III.

HOW TO TRAIN UP A PARENT IN THE WAY HE SHOULD GO.

III.

HOW TO TRAIN UP A PARENT IN THE WAY HE SHOULD GO.

"OH dear! I'm afraid I shall never manage to bring up my mother properly," was the remark once made by a rather fast young lady, to whom the old-fashioned institution of "mothers" was no doubt a rather inconvenient thing.

"My friend," said an old Quaker to a lady who contemplated adopting a child, "I know not how far thou wilt succeed in educating her, but I am quite certain she will educate thee."

Often when I look round on the world of parents and children, I think of those two contradictory speeches, and of the truth that lies between both.

The sentiment may be very heretical, but I

have often wondered how many out of the thousands of children born annually in our England alone, come to parents who at all deserve the blessing ? Not one-half, certainly—even among the mothers. Halve that again, and I believe you will come to the right per-centage as regards the fathers.

It is sometimes said that children of the present day are made too much of. Perhaps so. They but follow the fashion of the age—anything but a heroic or ascetic age. No doubt they are a little "spoiled." So are we all. But the errors of the parents, from which theirs arise, are a much more serious matter. How to train up the parents in the way they should go, is a necessity which, did it force itself upon the mind of any school board, would be found quite as important as the education of the children.

When we think of them, poor helpless little creatures ! who never asked to be born, who from birth upwards are so utterly dependent upon the two other creatures to whom they owe their existence—a debt for which it is supposed they can never be sufficiently grateful—do not our hearts yearn over them with pity, or grow hot with indignation? This even without need of such stories as we are continually hearing—I take three at random from to-day's newspaper—of the drunken father who amused himself with dashing his three-years-old child against the table till he accidentally dashed out its brains; of the woman who thrice in one afternoon tried to drop her baby among the horses and carriages in High Holborn; of the boy of four and a half flogged almost to death by a school-board teacher for not doing his sums and not answering when spoken to; which case the magistrate —doubtless himself a father—curtly dismissed, saying, "If discipline were not to be maintained, what was the education of boys to come to?"

However, putting aside these public facts, let us come upon our own private experience, and ask ourselves honestly, how many people we know who are—or are likely to prove—really good fathers and mothers? wise, patient, judicious; firm, watchful, careful, and loving? Above all things, just; since, so deeply is implanted in the infant mind this heavenly instinct, that if I were asked what was most important in the bringing up of a child, love or justice, I think I should say justice.

To be just is the very first lesson that a parent requires to learn. The rights of the little soul, which did not come into the world of its own accord, nor indeed was taken into consideration in the matter at all—for do any in marrying ever think of the sort of fathers or mothers they are giving to their offspring?—the rights of this offspring, physical, mental, and moral, are at once most obvious and least regarded. The new-born child is an interest, a delight, a pride; the parents exult over it, as over any other luxury or amusement; but how seldom do they take to heart the solemn responsibility of it, or see a face divine, as it were, looking out at them from the innocent baby-face, with the warning of Christ Himself—" Whosoever shall offend one of these little ones, it were better for him that a mill-stone were hung about his neck, and that he were cast into the sea."

There could hardly be a stronger expression

of the way in which God—the Christian God—
views the relation between parents and children.
Yet most young parents, who until now have
been accustomed to think only of themselves or
of one another, take the introduction of the
unconscious third as their natural possession,
never doubting that it is wholly theirs, to bring
up as they please, and that they are quite
capable of so doing.

Constantly one hears the remark, "Oh! I would
not take the responsibility of another person's
child." Does that imply that they feel at liberty
to do as they like with their own? I fear it
does; and that law and custom both appear to
sanction this delusion. Nobody must "interfere"
between parent and child, at least not till the
case comes within a degree or two of child-
murder. The slow destruction of soul and body
which, through ignorance or carelessness, goes
on among hundreds of children, not only in
humble, but in many respectable and well-
regulated households, society never notices. I
suppose even the most daring philanthropist
uld never venture to bring in a bill for claiming

the children of unworthy parents, and snatching them from ruin by annihilating all parental rights and making them children of the State. Yet such a proceeding would benefit the new generation to an incalculable degree.

"Train up a child in the way he should go," is the advice in everybody's mouth, but who thinks of training the parents? Does not everybody strictly hold that the mere fact of parenthood implies all that is necessary for the upbringing of the child?—all the love, all the wisdom, all the self-denial? Does it ever occur to the average young man and young woman, bending together over the cradle of their first-born, that the little thing, whose teachers they are proudly constituting themselves to be, is much more likely to be the unconscious agent in teaching them?

And the education begins at once. How amusing, and, at the same time, how satisfactory it is, to see a young fellow, who throughout his bachelor days has been a selfish egotist—most young bachelors are—obliged now to think of something and somebody besides himself; to give up not a few of his own personal comforts, and find himself forced to play second fiddle in his own home—where the one important object, for the time being, is "the baby."

I have spoken of rights. This is the only instance I know in which they are not mutual, but entirely one-sided. The new-born babe owes absolutely nothing to the parents beyond the physical fact of existence. All moral claims are on its side alone. The parents are responsible for it, soul and body, for certainly the first twenty years; nor, even after that, is it easy to imagine circumstances which could wholly set them free. The most sorely tried father and mother could hardly cast adrift their erring offspring, without a lurking uneasiness of conscience as to how far these errors were owing to themselves and their upbringing. For, save in very rare cases, where far-back types crop out again, and are most difficult to deal with, there is seldom a "black sheep" in any family without the parents having been to blame.

"Why, I brought up my children all alike," moans some virtuous progenitor of such. "How does it happen that this one has turned out so different from the rest?"

Just, my good friend, because you did bring them up all alike. You had not the sense to see that the same training which makes one mars another; or else that, in training them, it was necessary to train yourself first. Meaning to be a guide, you were only a finger-post, which points the way to others, but stands still itself.

The very first lesson a parent has to learn is, that whatever he attempts to teach, he must himself first practise. Whatever he wishes his child to avoid, he must make up his mind to renounce; and that from the very earliest stage of existence, and down to the minutest things.. In young children, the imitative faculty is so enormous, the reasoning power so small, that one cannot be too careful, even with infants, to guard against indulging in a harsh tone, a brusque manner, a sad or angry look. As far as is possible, the tender bud should live in an atmosphere of continual sunshine, under which it may safely and happily unfold, hour by hour, and day by day. To effect this there is required from the parent, or those who stand in the parent's stead, an amount of self-control and self-denial which would be almost impossible, had not Heaven implanted on the one side maternal instinct, on the other that extraordi-- nary winning charm which there is about all young creatures, making us put up with their endless waywardness, and love them all the better the more trouble they give us.

That is—mothers do. When I said "maternal instinct," I spoke advisedly and intentionally. Of paternal instinct there is almost none. A man is proud of his sons and daughters because they are *his* sons and daughters—bound to carry down his name to posterity; but he rarely takes the slightest interest in anybody else's children, and in his own only so far as they contribute to his pleasure, amusement, or dignity. The passionate love a woman often has for an- other woman's children, and for the feeblest, naughtiest, ugliest of her own, is to men a thing entirely unknown. Two-thirds of paternal love is pure pride, and the remaining third, not seldom, pure egotism.

Therefore, for the first seven, nay ten years of a child's life, it should in most cases be left as much as possible to the care of women. Not that every woman has the motherly heart; but the fatherly heart is a rarer thing still.

Besides, men's work in the world naturally unfits them for the management of children. It is very hard for a man, who has been worried in business all day long, to come home and be pestered by a crying child; even though the poor innocent cannot help itself—is probably only tired, or sick, or hungry. But the father will not see this; he will only see that the child annoys himself, and must therefore be " naughty."

" And when naughty, of course it must be punished," I heard a middle-aged father once say with virtuous complacency. " My boy is only eleven months old—yet I assure you I have whipped him three times."

Whipped him three times! And the mother allowed it,—the young mother who sat smiling and beautifully dressed at the head of the table. Why had she not the sense to lock her nursery door against the brutal fool? But what is the good of calling names? the man was simply ignorant. For all his grand assumption of parental authority, he had not the wit to see that for the first year, perhaps two years of our life, there can be no such thing as moral "naughtiness." Existence is so purely physical that if we only take care of the little body, the mind will take care of itself; or, at worst, it is so completely a piece of white paper, that it will show nothing save what we write upon it. Anybody who has had much to do with young children must acknowledge that, in spite of the doctrine of original sin, nearly every childish fault is a reflected fault, the copy of something seen in other people. If any one will take the trouble to notice his own faults or peculiarities—which we are all rather slow to do—it may account for a good many "naughtinesses" which he punishes in his offspring.

It is often strange and sad to see how hard grown-up people—especially men — are upon children : expecting from five—or say ten years old — an amount of patience, diligence, self-control and self-denial which they themselves, at fifty odd, have never succeeded in attaining to. But I repeat, so few men are by temperament, circumstances, or habits in the least fitted for the management of children, that the advice I give to all sensible wives and capable mothers concerning their little ones, is this—"Save their fathers from them, and save them from their fathers."

Not but that there are fathers true and tender, firm as a man ought to be, unselfish and patient as, happily, most women are; to whose breast the youngest child runs to in any trouble, "Oh, it's always papa who comforts us," and of whom the elder ones say fondly, "We mind one look of papa's more than twenty scoldings." But such are the exceptions. The average of men and fathers are, I solemnly believe, quite unfitted, both by nature or habit, for the upbringing of children. Thus, necessarily the duty falls on the mother. And why not? What higher destiny?

There is a class of women who consider that they have a higher destiny; that to help in the larger work of the world, to continue their own mental culture, is far more important than to bring up the next generation worthily.

Both duties are excellent in their way; but there are plenty of unmarried childless women, and women with no domestic instincts, to do the former: mothers alone can do the latter. True, it exacts the devotion of the entire life; a real mother has no time for gay society, nor intellectual development, except such as she is always gaining through her children; she must make up her mind to the fact that they and her husband compose her world, and fill up her life.

And what better world? what nobler life? Even if she is worn out, " like a rose-tree in full bearing," and drops off when her destiny is done. No matter, she has fulfilled it, and she is and she will be blessed.

Not, however, unless she has thoroughly fulfilled it. The mere fact of bringing eight or ten children into the world does not in the least imply true motherhood. If she leaves them to nurses and governesses; if she shirks any of the anxious cares, perpetual small worries, and endless self-abnegations which are her natural portion, the under-side to her infinite blessings, she does not deserve these last. Not every mother is born with the mother's heart: I have known many an old maid who had it, and I have heard of mothers of many children who owned to "hating" every child as it came, and only learning to love the helpless innocent from a sense of duty. But duty often teaches love, and responsibility produces the capacity for it. Many a light-minded, light-hearted girl, who has danced and flirted and sentimentalised through her happy spring-time, finds the sweet compulsion of nature too strong for her: very soon she forgets all her follies, and settles down into a real mother, whom love instructs in all things necessary; who shrinks from no trouble, is equal to all duties; is to her children nurse, companion, playfellow, as well as doctress, sempstress, teacher, friend. Everything, in short. The father may be more or less to the child, as his occupation and his own peculiarities allow; but the mother *must* be all in all, or God help the children!

Granting that the mother-love is there, is love sufficient? Not always. It will not make up for the lack of common sense, self-control, accurate and orderly ways;

> " The reason firm, the temperate will ;
> Endurance, foresight, strength, and skill."

Nor does the mere fact of parenthood by a sort of divine right constitute all parents infallible, as they are so apt to suppose, and by their conduct expect their children to believe it.

The child will *not* believe it, not after the very first, unless the parent proves it; and this by something stronger than bare assertion or natural instinct. It may be a dangerous thing to suggest, but I am afraid the idea of some mysterious instinctive bond between parent and child is a mere superstition. No doubt the feeling is there, but it may be exercised equally with or without the tie of blood. Suppose, unknown to these tender young parents, another infant, a " changeling child," were to be secretly popped into the cradle over which they bend so fondly? They would feel towards it exactly the same sensations.   Also, if any aunt, grandmother, or even ordinary stranger should fulfil towards that child all the duties of a parent, the love won, and deserved, would be a true filial affection.   The instinct of blood, as people call it, acts admirably as a cement to other ties ; but of itself, save in poetical fancy, it has no existence whatever.   Nothing but the wildest imagination could have made George Eliot's " Spanish Gipsy," tenderly reared and betrothed to the man she loved, elope at once with her Zingaro father, whom she had never seen in her life before.   And nothing but the most extraordinary moral twist could make people condemn, as I have heard condemned, Silas Marner's beloved Eppie, because, placed between her adopted father, to whom she owed everything, and her flesh-and-blood father, to whom she owed nothing but her birth, she never hesitated in choosing the former.

A parent, unlike a poet, is not born, he is made.   There are certain things which he has at once to learn, or he will have no more influence over his child than if he were a common stranger. First, he must institute between himself and his child that which is as important between child and parent as between man and God—the sense, not of absolute obedience, as is so often preached, but of absolute reliance, which produces obedience. To gain obedience, you must first set yourself to deserve it. Whatever you promise your little one, however small the thing may seem to you, and whatever trouble it costs you, perform it. Never let the doubt once enter that innocent mind, that you say what you do not mean, or will not act up to what you say. Make as few prohibitory laws as you possibly can, but once made, keep to them. In what is granted, as in what is denied, compel yourself, however weary, or worried, or impatient, to administer always even-handed justice. "Fiat justitia, ruat cœlum," is a system much more likely to secure your child's real affection than all the petting and humouring so generally indulged in, to give pleasure or save trouble, not to your little ones, but to yourself.

A very wise woman once consoled an over-tender mother, who was being blamed for "spoiling" her little girl, "Never mind. Love never spoiled any child. It is the alternations, the kiss on the one cheek and the blow on the other, which ruin."

And this is what I often notice in extremely well-meaning parents; their love is not a steady love, but continually

> "Roughened by those cataracts and breaks,
> Which humour interposed too often makes."

They cannot keep that sweet, level calm which above all things is necessary for the government of children. The same playful wiles which amuse one day, irritate the next. Not that the child is different, but they are in a different mood themselves, which important fact the poor little thing is expected at once to recognise, and act accordingly.

And here the second great mistake is made. We expect too much from our children. We exact from them a perfection which we are far from carrying out in ourselves; we require of them sacrifices much heavier, comparatively, than those of any grown-up person. And they soon find out that. A child's eyes are very sharp.

Any flaw in one's argument, any lapse in one's conduct, is caught up by them and reproduced with alarming accuracy.

"Mr. A. ; is that the Mr. A. whom papa dislikes so?" said an innocent "enfant terrible" before a whole dinner-table. And papa, who had let his prejudices run away with him, so as to speak a great deal more strongly than he meant of harmless Mr. A., felt that after this there would be some difficulty in teaching his child to obey the ninth commandment and bear no false witness against its neighbour.

The intense truthfulness and straight-forwardness of children, when not crushed by fear, or corrupted by precocious deceit, is a perpetual lesson to elder people, who have learnt to disguise their feelings ; as, I suppose, we all must, in degree.

"Mamma, I don't like that gentleman ; when is he going away?" observed the same painfully candid child, concerning a morning visitor, who had the grace to say politely, "My dear, I am going away directly," and disappear. But then it was necessary to take the matter in hand.

And never, perhaps, did the mother feel so strongly that courtesy is a Christian virtue, and Christian charity the basis of all good-breeding, than when she had to explain to her little daughter that it was not "kind" to make such a remark; that whether we like people or not, whether they are agreeable or disagreeable, we are equally bound to show them civility, since by incivility we disgrace not them, but ourselves. And this without advocating any insincerity, or hypocrisy, or even "company manners," which no child is ever likely to assume, except in imitation of its elders.

To be perfectly true, perfectly just, perfectly loving to our children, is the only way of teaching them to be the same to other people. The very tone of voice, the turn of phrase, the trick of manner of their elders and (so-called) superiors are often imitated by them with such a frightful accuracy that it is necessary to be continually on our guard. One sees one's own reflection in these awful little people as startlingly as if one were living in a room of looking-glasses. And therein lies the continual education which, whether or not the parent gives to the child, the child unconsciously gives to the parent. Happy he who is clear-sighted enough to read the lesson, and wise enough to profit thereby.

On this head let me suggest, that if the children miss much, the parents miss more, by the fashion—exacted, I suppose, by the ever-growing luxuriousness of our middle classes—of keeping children so much in the nursery, and under an array of nursemaids. Yet I have heard very sensible mothers advocate this; declaring that it "rests" the little brain to be left to the company of servants.

Our neighbours across the Channel think differently. In French domestic life—provincial life, for France is even more distinct from Paris than England from London—in that cheerful, affectionate, happy home life which is, I believe, far commoner with them than with us, one of the brightest and most wholesome elements is the children. They have no nursery, and, after the very earliest infancy, they have no *bonne.* The little people are always with the big people

—father and mother, grandfather and grand-mother—for the French household is often made up of several generations. As soon as they can sit at table, they take their place there; in the *salon* they are as welcome as in the *salle-à-manger ;* and thus, unconsciously brought into training by the good manners of those about them, they learn to be little ladies and gentle-men almost before they can speak.

"But," I have heard people argue, "how can you possibly have children always beside you? As babies you might, if you could put up with the trouble of them; but when they grow older it would be so very awkward. For their own sakes even, you ought not to let them hear their elders' conversation."

What an admission! Does it occur to any of these arguers that, except in very rare and solemn instances, the talk which is unfit for the ears of children ought never to be talked at all? For what does it usually consist of? Criticizing one's neighbours; sneering at one's friends; ridiculing behind their backs those whom we praise to their faces; telling secrets which ought never to be told; making bitter, or equivocal, or ill-natured remarks, which we are afraid to hear repeated. If so, to keep our children always in the room would be a very wholesome discipline, making us much better folks than some of us are now.

Not that I by any means wish to take a sentimental or picturesque view of the rising generation. It is often a very aggravating generation indeed. Without any actual naughtiness, the restlessness which is natural to a child—indeed, a portion of its daily growth—is most trying to elder people, who have come to feel the intense blessedness of mere rest. And when it becomes worse than recklessness—actual wilfulness and mischievousness—even the strongest opponents, theoretically, of corporal chastisement, will at times feel their fingers tingling with an irresistible inclination to box their darling's ears.

The more reason, therefore, that they should restrain themselves, and not do it. For punishment is not for the good of the punisher, but the punished; and no punishment inflicted in a moment of irritation can ever be of the smallest good to either side.

And this brings us to a widely discussed question;—whether corporal punishment should ever be inflicted on children. For me, I answer decidedly, Never!

My reasons are these. To the very young— the eleven months' old infant, for instance— such a chastisement is simply brutal; to a child old enough to understand the humiliation of it, a whipping can rarely do good, and may do incalculable harm. Besides, the degradation rests not alone with the child. A big creature beating a little one is always in a position very undignified, to say the least of it. Also, there is a certain difficulty in making the victim comprehend, that the same line of conduct which his parents exercise towards him is utterly forbidden him to exercise towards his younger brothers and sisters.

It is possible, I grant, that there may be cases of actual moral turpitude—lying, theft, and the like—when nothing short of physical punishment will affect the culprit, and the parent has to stand forth as the stern administrator of justice; but it must be clearly shown to be justice, not revenge. I have known men so self-controlled, so tender, and withal so unswervingly just, that the inevitable whipping being inflicted, and submitted to, with a mournful solemnity, the instant it was over the boy's arms were round the father's neck, and both wept together. But such cases are so exceptional, that they cannot be taken as a guide. The ordinary rule is, that when a child is bad enough to deserve a whipping, the infliction of it will likely only harden him ; and if he does not deserve it, his whole nature will revolt in fury at the punishment.

I shall never forget once seeing a small boy of ten, the inheritor of his father's violent temper, whom that father, for some trivial fault, seized and struck. The little fellow raised himself on tiptoe, and, doubling his small fist, with all his might and main struck back again. A proceeding which so astonished the father— who, like all tyrants, was rather a coward—that he shrank back, and retired from the field. He hated his boy ever after, but he never more attempted to thrash him.

You will perceive I hold that, in the training of the young, example is everything, precept almost nothing. Half the good advice we give, certainly more than half of our scolding, just "goes in at one ear and out at the other." The continual reproach of, "You naughty child!" the seldom-fulfilled threat of, "I'll punish you!" come in time to fall quite harmless upon hardened ears. But a child to whom fear is absolutely unknown — as unknown as punishment—whose naughtiness is met solely by silence, feels this silence alone to be the most terrible retribution for ill-doing. The withdrawal of the parent's smile is to it like the hiding of God's face. "Oh, mamma, don't look so! I can't bear it. It kills me!" is the cry of such a child, falling on its bended knees in an agony of contrition and tears.

It is not the preaching, not the teaching, not the continual worry of, "Don't do that!" "Why didn't you do this?" which makes children what we call "good" children; that is, honest, truth-

ful, obedient; troublesome, perhaps—all children are troublesome—but guilty of no mean-
ness, deceitfulness, or wilful mischievousness.
It is the constant living example of those they
are with. They get into the habit of being
"good," which makes this line of conduct so
natural that they never think of any other.

And here we come upon another moot question ;—whether or not there should be exacted
from children blind obedience? Sometimes,
perhaps; there may be cases where such is
the only safety. But ordinarily speaking,
while, as I have said, a child's first lesson
should be trained into that implicit reliance
on the parent which of necessity induces obedience, I think the parent ought to be exceedingly cautious how he exacts this obedience
without giving a sufficient reason for it. At
an incredibly early age the reasoning powers
of a child can be developed, if the parent will
take a little trouble to do it; and how very
much trouble it saves afterwards he will soon
find out. Three words of gentle explanation—
"Don't do that, my child, because," &c., &c.

—will give him a stronger influence, a completer authority, over the little mind than any
harshly iterated, unexplained prohibitions. And
the good of this works both ways; while it
gives the child confidence in the parent, it
teaches the parent his most difficult part, to
exercise authority without tyranny. That bar-
baric dictum, "Do this, because I choose it,"
becomes softened into the Christian command,
"Do this, because I wish it," or the still higher
law, "because it is right." I have never yet
known a child "naughty" enough deliberately
to refuse to do a thing, when asked to do it
simply on the ground "that it was right."

This, again, leads us to a point upon which I
think many, nay, most parents grievously err—
the system of rewards and punishments. It is
like bringing into innocent child-life that terrible creed which makes religion consist, not in
the love of God, and the obeying Him because
we love Him, but in finding out the best and
easiest way to take care of ourselves—to keep
out of hell and get into heaven.

A principle which, put thus into plain English,

we start at, yet whether or not believing in it ourselves, we practise it fatally with our children. " Do this, and I'll give you such and such a thing." "Dare to do that, and I will take from you so and so, which you delight in." A method which, like some forms of theology, may be convenient and effective at the time, but which afterwards is most ruinous, inasmuch as it entirely abrogates that doctrine upon which I base the whole mutual training of parents and children —the doctrine of absolute right for right's sake.

For how, if you have brought up young creatures on the principle of " Behave well, and you shall have a sweetie "—" Behave ill, and I'll whip you or send you to bed," can you follow it out by teaching your growing boy or girl to " eschew evil and do good " purely for the love of good and the hatred of evil? How, above all, can you put into their hearts the love of God, when in after-life He hides His face in so many dark ways—when His teachings seem often so mysterious, nay, cruel—except by saying, " Love Him because He is perfect Love—adore Him, because He is absolute justice " ?

Next to that justice, which is, I believe, a heavenly instinct with almost all young children, their strongest need, and the most powerful influence with them, is sympathy. And this the wise parent will give at all times and under all circumstances. A child accustomed to find in the mother's bosom a perpetual refuge, to bring there all its little woes—so small to us, to it so large—to get answers to all its questions, interest in all its discoveries, sympathy in all its amusements; over a child so trained the influence of the mother is enormous, nay, unlimited. What a safeguard to both! not only in childhood, but in after-years. To feel that she is an absolute providence to her child— that from babyhood it has clung to the simple belief that mamma must be told everything, and can right everything. What an incalculable blessing! lasting till death, and after—the remembrance of a mother from whom the child has never received anything but love!

Love, the root of sympathy, is the most powerful agent in the bringing up of children. Not mere caresses; yet these are not to be despised, as being "the outward and visible sign of an inward and spiritual grace." The earliest development of our nature is so entirely objective rather than subjective, practical rather than ethical, that a kiss or a cuddle at all times is a much more potent agent in moral education than stern elder folk believe. Love, not in word only, but in action ; love, ever at hand to remove small evils, to lessen great ones ; to answer all questions, and settle all difficulties ; to be a refuge in trouble, a sharer in joy, and a court of appeal where there is always certainty of sympathy if not redress ; this is the sort of thing which gives to parents their highest, noblest influence —beginning with birth and ending only with the grave.

An influence which alone can knit anew the parental and filial tie at the time—and this time comes in all lives—when it is so apt to loosen ; I mean when the child, which at first had seemed a mere mirror reflecting the objects placed before it, develops into an individual character, sometimes a character as different as possible from both father and mother.

This is a hard crisis, common though it be. Fathers who see their boys growing up without a single habit or taste resembling their own, mothers who perplexedly trace in their young daughters some type of womanhood totally distinct from, and perhaps very distasteful to, themselves, are surely much to be pitied. But so are the children, especially those who, with their originality, impetuosity, and passionate impulses after unknown good, have all the ignorance of youth concerning the known good—the patience, the wisdom, the long-suffering, which is, or ought to be, the strongest characteristic of parents.

It has been learned by them through years of sore teaching. That perpetual self-denial, which, as I have said, begins at the very cradle—that habit of instinctively thinking, in all things great and small, not of their own pleasure, not even of their child's pleasure, but of that child's ultimate good—has been in all parents who really deserve the name a training they can never forget. It helps them now, in this difficult time, which, I repeat, comes soon or late in almost all families; when there is a grand clashing of rights and conflict of duties, occasionally ending in a general upbreaking of both.

A child's first rights are, I have said, plain enough; as plain as the parent's duties. Afterwards they become less clear. The extent to which a parent should put up with a child, or a child withstand a parent, is most difficult to decide. Equally difficult is it to say how far both are right or both wrong, in the sad season when one side becomes exacting and the other careless; when, despite all outward show of respect and affection, the father feels indignantly that his influence over his boys is almost nothing, and the mother, with a sharp pang at her heart, which she vainly tries to hide, is conscious that her young daughter, who for twenty years has been the delight of her eyes, prefers being the delight of other eyes, and, though very kind to her, finds her—just a little uninteresting.

The time—it must come to us all—when we cease to be a sort of lesser providence to our children, who cease in their turn to look up to us and lean all their troubles upon us; when they begin to think and act for themselves, and, quite unconsciously perhaps, put us a little on one side as old, and odd, and out of date; unquestionably this is a bitter climax to our years of patient love. Yet it is but a portion of the training—usually the highest and best training we ever get—which God gives to us through our children. And it is not impossible to be passed through, and safely, too, on both sides; especially in families which have been brought up on the principle I have before upheld—of absolute right, to be followed without regard to either benefit or injury, pleasure or pain.

The doctrine with which I started—of the child's claims upon the parent being far stronger than those of the parent upon the child—teaches us, to the very last, at least tolerance. If our sons resist us in choosing a career, or, still worse, in choosing companions that we believe will ruin that career—if our daughters will go and fall in love with the last men in the world we would have desired for their husbands—well, why is this? These young souls were given to us apparently an absolute blank page, upon which we might write what we chose. We have written. It is we who have formed their characters, guided their education, governed their morals. Everything they are now we have or are supposed to have made them ; at least, we once thought we should be able to make them. If they turn out well we shall assuredly take the credit of it ; if they turn out ill—what say we then ? That it is their fault, or ours ?

As a general rule, if, as soon as time has enabled our sons and daughters to escape out of our authority, they escape out of our influence also—if, having ceased to rule, we have no power to guide—there must be something wrong somewhere ; somebody has been to blame. Can it possibly be ourselves ?

The system that prevention is better than cure, is infallible with little children—no one doubts that. Any parents who for want of rational precaution allowed their children to fall into the fire or the water, or to do one another some serious bodily harm, would be stigmatized as either wicked or insane. Yet, when the young people are growing up—and just at the most critical point of their lives—how often do these parents shut the stable door *after* the steed is stolen!

"Sir," said a shrewd old gentlemen, when questioned as to the character of one of his guests—"Sir, do you think I would ever let a young man inside my doors who was not fit to marry my daughter?"

And the same principle might apply to sons: not only as to their marriage—which is a later affair, and one which after all they must settle for themselves—but as far as possible with regard to their ordinary associates and associations. Even as a wise mother makes her nursery one of the cheerfullest rooms in the house, a wise father will in after-years try to make his house one of the pleasantest places in the world to his grown-up sons—a home from which they will never care long to stray, and to which they will look back, amidst the storms of the world, as a happy haven, where was neither dulness nor harshness; where the reins of authority were prudently and slowly relaxed, until nothing remained of the necessary absolute control of childhood, save the tender reasoning—" for your own good, my boy "—which boys so seldom fully prize until they have it no longer.

Girls too, who may have lovers in plenty, but have only one mother; perhaps some of them think, or have once thought, that a mother's sympathy and advice is the most intolerable thing imaginable in love-affairs, which generally between parents and children are one long worry from beginning to end. This, even when the end is happy marriage. But how often do we see parents looking irritably or anxiously upon a long string of unmarried daughters, wondering mournfully what in the world is to become of them by-and-by?

And here I must give utterance to another heresy. I think we English parents do not take half enough trouble to marry our children—that is, to give them fair opportunity of marriage. We are so apt to consider them exclusively our own property, and to feel personally aggrieved when they wish to strike into new ground, or form new ties for themselves. Or else we are weary and lazy; life is not to us what it once

was—what it now is to them ; we prefer to sit
at ease by the fireside ; visitors rather trouble
us ; we grudge our young people the society they
naturally crave for, and in which, rationally
guided, they would find their best chance of
choice.

Consequently, our sons often make rash
mistakes in marriage—and our daughters not
unfrequently do not marry at all. This is no
dire misfortune. Anything less than a thoroughly
happy marriage is to women much worse than
celibacy ; but still it is a sad thing to parents to
watch a family of girls " withering on the virgin
thorn," with no natural outlet for their affections ; themselves a little soured and their elders
just a little disappointed ; for no doubt there is a
certain dignity in " my married daughter,"
perhaps as being an unconscious tribute from
the son-in-law to the parent of his wife, never
attained by the mother of unappreciated old
maids.

If foreign parents are to be blamed for the
"arranged" or compelled marriages which we in
free England so strongly condemn, I think we

are also to blame when we either deliberately stand in the way of our children's happiness, or tacitly let it slip by, giving them no opportunity of making a rational choice in marriage. Surely it is the bounden duty of wise elders not to ignore nature, but to accept the inevitable cares of " pairing-time," when the young birds, fully fledged, will desire to leave the nest, however soft it is made ; when that overpowering instinct before which the warmest filial love sinks cold and colourless, will assert itself, ay, and guide itself too ; unless we have strength and self-denial—ah, no end to parental self-denial!—to forget our personal pain, and throwing ourselves heartily into the young folks' place, succeed in guiding it a little also.

At best, this love-season is a sad one, since few love-affairs are perfectly smooth and happy, and to see our children suffer is sharper than to suffer ourselves ; especially when we can no longer help them. While they are babies, there is a certain omnipotence about parenthood ; but when the time comes that the child's unfailing shelter is no longer the mother's heart, when the father's strong right arm of guidance and protection sinks absolutely powerless—then things grow hard.

Harder still, when, as sometimes happens, the parents' will pulls one way and the child's another. One side or other must yield. It is the last and sorest lesson in the parents' training, to feel that in most cases it is they who will have to yield.

I do not uphold marriages against the consent of parents. I believe they never happen without something a little wrong on both sides; and when they do happen, they always bring with them their punishment—to both. This, even when things smooth down, as they most often do. But the act itself remains, and the result of it—even as I heard a young daughter lately protest, when her lover was interdicted the house—" Why do you blame me, mamma? You married papa in direct opposition to *your* parents."

And this must sometimes be done. Both the laws of our country, and the honest moral sense thereof, allow it. Abroad, it is more difficult. But here in England, after the age of twenty-one, any young man or woman may deliberately walk out of the father's house and into the nearest church, and be married to whom he or she pleases. But, I think, the only permissible way of so doing lies in doing it thus openly and deliberately, and after all rational submission and persuasion have failed. Such a marriage cannot be a happy thing ; it will be a sore thing in many ways to all parties, as long as they live. But it may be a necessary and not unrighteous thing, and it may turn out a portion of that salutary training which is given us, not by our children, but by heaven, through them.

Looking at things in this light, we can better learn to bear the griefs and perplexities of that troublous time to which I am referring. It may be lightened, if we take care to keep for our grown-up sons and daughters the same key which unfailingly unlocked the baby-heart—sympathy. A broken doll—a broken heart—has not the mother's heart balm for both ? That is, if we still have strength not to think of ourselves

first, but of our children. Above all, not to be
vexed or irritated, as we sometimes are, even at
their happiness. For under the most favourable
circumstances, what son ever brought to his
mother a daughter whom she really considered
worthy of him? And what father ever gave his
consent to the addresses of the most unexcep-
tionable of sons-in-law, without a secret wish
to shut the door in his face?

Yes, there may be wounds—there must be;
but they will not be poisoned wounds, if the
parents have done their duty. And by-and-by
the reward will come, if reward ever does come,
as a complete thing, or is ever meant to do so,
in this world. Certainly not parental reward.
If parents work for that they will fail. " Take
this child and nurse it *for Me*"—is God's command concerning every little soul put into life.
How few parents either hear, believe, or obey
it, He knows.

Yet the truth remains a truth still, and likewise a consolation. Even as a young mother
sees, and will often have to see, her little one
turn from her to some more amusing person,

who perhaps is less strict, less wise, merely thinking of her or his own pleasure with the child, and not the child's real good ; so many a mother, well on in years, may have to be taught the sad but wholesome lesson that her children were not merely *her* children, made exactly after her pattern, and bound to minister solely to her comfort and carry out her wishes, but were also meant to be, so to speak, the children of heaven. If they continue such, living out their life in righteous and honourable fashion, even though it may not be her life, nor carried out after her fashion—still, she will accept the will of heaven, and learn to be content. The mental training has been gone through ; she has educated her children, and they have educated her; all may not be perfectly smooth and happy, but still all is well.

Every mother must be in degree a sort of Hannah. She may bring her son his little coat—she may come up to see him yearly in the temple ; but with all that she must give him to God. To give our children up to God, to end with a training totally different from that with

K

which we began, to be obliged to recognise our own powerlessness, and learn to sit still with folded hands, resigning them and their fortunes into their own hands—or rather into Higher hands than either theirs or ours—this is no easy lesson for parents. And yet we must learn it—the sharpest and the last.

No, not quite the last. As said a little girl of six—whose only idea of death was of "going up into the sky," and being made perfectly happy and lovely and good—after being taken to see an old woman of ninety-nine, "Oh, mamma, please don't live to be ninety-nine. You'll be so ugly!"

Alas, there comes a time when we know we must be "ugly," more or less; physically, and perhaps morally too; when the worn-out body will not respond to the mind, or, maybe, even the mind is wearing out, so that by no possibility can we give pleasure, and may give much pain, even to our best beloved.

This is a hard time; nor is it wonderful that parents and children sometimes succumb to it, and the relation, once so sweet and easy, becomes a heavy burden. But there are parents who make it much heavier than it need to be, by their extreme selfishness, their utter want of recognition of the fact that the most duteous child that ever was born cannot live for ever in a sick-room or beside an arm-chair. The younger life has to last long after the elder one is ended. To blight it, even for a time, by any unnecessary suffering is a cruelty, which not even the sternest upholder of filial duty can ever justify.

I have seen parents, not intentionally selfish, who, when old age came upon them, grew so exacting, fretful, irritable, compelled such constant attendance, and insisted on such incessant sacrifices, as literally to take the life—or at least all that life was worth—out of their children, whom everybody but themselves saw were being "killed by inches," as the phrase is. Only fancy! living till one's best friends say with bated breath, "If it would but come to an end"—that is, our life; as the only means of saving other and more precious lives.

But this need not be—it ought never to be.

A little self-control at the beginning, a steady, persistent recognition of the fact that the young are young, and we are old; they blooming, we fading; they going up the hill, and we down it —that this is God's will, to be accepted placidly and cheerfully, and made as little trouble about as possible, and we need not fear ever becoming very "ugly." Especially since, as the mother answered that little girl, we need not have much fear of living till ninety-nine.

But before the "ugly" time there is another, which must be rather sweet than sad—the silent time "between the lights"—when the labour of the day is over, and the rest of the night not yet come; when the house is empty of little feet and noisy tumultuous voices, and the parents, who once thought they would have given anything in the world for quiet, now have quiet enough; only too much perhaps. All the obstreperous young flock are grown up and gone away, some into married homes, some into the work of the busy world, some into a silenter world, where earthly work is over. And these, I think, are the only children parents keep *for ever*. The others come and go, returning to the old home merely for a little while; but still it is plain to see—often they allow it to be seen, a little too plainly—that the parents' house is their real home no more.

And so the two old folks—fortunate if there are still two—must learn to sit together by their silent fireside, remembering that they have but gone the way which their parents did before them, and their children must follow after; that all is quite natural, quite right, and there is nothing to complain of: only, sometimes, it feels just a little hard.

Or, it would feel hard, had we not strength to take in that consolation which I have spoken of—that our children are God's children as much as ours—lent, and not given. "Inasmuch as ye have done it unto the least of these, ye have done it unto Me."

And He never denies us the reward. It comes, in a certain degree, from the very first; for amidst the endless trouble they give, the almost unbearable trials to patience and temper that they bring, every child brings its own blessing likewise. A daily blessing—refreshing, soothing, cheering — for the companionship of an ordinarily good and intelligent boy or girl is often better than that of any grown-up person. And the love of a child, its absolute unshaken trust—when it has always met trust for trust, and love for love—how sweet both are! How perfect is the delight, the perfection of all human delights, of those years when parents have their little flock around them, and watch them grow up day by day, like the Holy Child of Nazareth— " in wisdom and in stature, and in favour with God and man."

There is a joy, greater than even the joy of a mother over her first-born, or the exultation of a man over the baby-son to whom he hopes to bequeath his honour, his worldly goods, and his unblemished name; and that is, to have arrived at old age and seen this child, from its own day of birth to its parents' death-day, living the life they would have it live, carrying out the principles they taught it, and being in every way what I have called "the child of

heaven "—God's child as well as theirs. Then,
all the training, bitter and sweet, which they
have undergone, and made their child undergo
—for no parents are worth the name who have
not strength sometimes to wring their own
hearts, and their child's too, for a good end—
will have been softened down into permanent
peace. A peace, enduring even amidst all the
trying weaknesses of old age, all the probable
sufferings of the failing body and worn-out
mind; lasting even to the supreme moment,
when the aged, dying head rests on the still
young breast, and the child kisses the closed
eyes, which, through all anxiety, pain, even
displeasure, never lost their look of love—never
till now. And now it is all ended.—No, not
ended—God forbid.

There was a parent I knew—one who had
been both father and mother to his children
(as some fathers can be, and are, thank God!)
for nearly half a century. Passing away, in the
ripe perfectness of a most noble life, he was
heard to whisper feebly, "Adieu, ma fille!"
She sobbed out, "Non, non, mon père!" He

lifted himself up in the bed, and with the old gleam in his eyes, the old force in his voice, to an extent of which those present had hardly believed a dying man capable, exclaimed, "Non, non. Pas adieu!—Au revoir!"

And surely if there are any meetings, any reunions granted in the other world, they will be granted to parents and children.

*   *   *   *   *   *

"Train up a parent in the way he should go," was the queer title I gave to this sermon. You may have begun it with a smile; perhaps you will have ended it, as I do, with something more like a tear. That is just what I meant. Farewell.

Sermon IV.

BENEVOLENCE—OR BENEFICENCE?

IV.

" I DO believe that one half the so-called 'charity' going is, in its results, worse than an error—an actual crime. Suppose you were to write an essay upon 'The Crime of Benevolence!'"

The arch-heretic who suggested this had been spurred on thereto by a recent visit to a very " benevolent " parish, probably one of the richest and most charitable parishes in the kingdom. It possessed—possesses still, for aught I know—within a very moderate area, not too densely populated, three churches, one chapel, and two iron rooms for mission services. It had clothing clubs, coal clubs, blanket clubs, provident and work societies. At its parish school an admirable education

could be got for threepence a week. Its penny
readings for the men, its mothers' meetings for
the women, gave every opportunity of mental
and moral improvement to that class which
we patronisingly term " our poorer brethren."
In short, everything was done that could be
done to make poverty unnecessary and vice
impossible.

Yet, my informant confessed, both abounded.
Public-houses stared you in the face at every
corner, and were always full—of women as
well as men. Consequently, wretched homes,
neglected children, young women whom no
wise mistress of a house ever thought of
taking into her service, middle-aged women
whom to employ as laundresses, sempstresses,
or even charwomen was hopeless—their characters were so bad. Even the long-suffering
clergymen's wives and district visitors, trying
continually to do good, were as continually
baffled. Nobody having once employed the
objects of their hopeless compassion, ever did it
again. Charity these people were always open
to receive, but the best kind of charity—work—

it was useless to give, if the giver wished it to be anything better than a disguised form of almsgiving.

And yet this place was an El Dorado of benevolence ; where the poor not only got their daily bread, but got it buttered on both sides. An opportune death, or fortunate accident, would bring to the spot half-a-dozen clergymen with prayers and purses, half-a-dozen ladies following with tracts and clothes; until the sufferers, becoming quite important people, realised fully the advantage of being " afflicted," and continuing to be. One story I heard of a labourer's household, which, deprived suddenly of its drunken head, found itself "assisted" so much, that when it went to church next Sunday in its new clothes, a shrewd neighbour declared it reminded her of Mrs. Hofland's tale, "The Clergyman's widow, and her young family." And the youngest child being met afterwards, "Yes, ma'am," said the mother, in a whining tone, "I've just been taking Bobby to the doctor, and he orders him wine," with a glance that, meeting no response, dropped immediately. But the habit of begging was too strong to be resisted. "Do you think, ma'am," with an additional whine of humility, "you've got such a thing as a pot of strawberry jam for Bobby to take his physic in?"

It is these sort of people who harden one's heart, and incline one to rank our benevolent friends with two other classes, equally injurious —I was going to write obnoxious—the folk who pride themselves on the fact that if they have a fault, it is being too "tender-hearted;" and those weak fools, the scourge and torment of society, who are politely said to be "nobody's enemy but their own."

To call benevolence a crime! To say that benevolent people actually injure those they attempt to aid! It seems a curious paradox; but does not experience prove it to be very near the truth? And why?

This question is best answered by another. What is benevolence? Literally, the word means "wishing well," and I suppose we must take for granted that all benevolence really wishes well to its object; that is, it would rather do good than not, provided the thing costs little trouble. Beyond that—well, let any one of us try honestly, as honestly as if we all lived in the Palace of Truth, to analyze the motive of his next act of charity; say, the next sixpence he gives to a street-beggar.

Why does he give it? First, probably, to save himself pain. It is decidedly painful to look upon distress, and troublesome to be followed down the street with whining petitions for aid. Also, a kind action gratifies our self-love, and makes us generally comfortable ; and to be thanked is more than comfortable—agreeable. So he extracts the coin from his pocket, throws it to the beggar, and goes his way ; but of the various complex motives for this benevolent action, almost all concern not the object of it, but his own self. Except, indeed, the natural motive of all benevolence, for which we ought in justice to give all benevolent people the credit, a general kindly feeling to their species, and a wish to benefit them rather than do them harm. But the question—just as I argued in relation to self-sacrifice — whether the important element in a gift is the advantage of the donor or the recipient, does not occur to them.

Not, when the good deed is private and small, like the eleemosynary sixpence referred to : still less when the benevolence is public; say, a church collection when the churchwarden, our neighbour and friend, is holding the plate; or a subscription to a charity, in which everybody will see our name, and the sum appended thereto.

Now I do not mean to be severe upon the many rich people in our rich England, whose purses are always open to public or private charity. They do their duty. Society expects it of them, and they know it does. Besides, they really like to do good, and the easiest way of doing it is through their pockets. Any other way takes such a world of trouble ; and they dislike trouble,—most people do. They give— to anybody or anything—of what costs them nothing, and which they never miss. They enjoy all the credit of doing a generous action, and the burden of really doing it falls upon other people. What matter? they argue; it is only division of labour. So others do the work, and they the magnificence. It is so easy to be magnificent, when one is either a spendthrift or a millionaire. The difference looks very small; only a word, or a few letters in a word; yet, if we examine it, it is enormous. It is the difference between Benevolence and Beneficence.

An extravagant person may be as extravagant in his charities as he is in his luxuries; for charity is, in truth, a sort of luxury. Many a man called benevolent is simply wasteful, and the cause of waste in others; for to give away money without considering how far the recipient has a right to it, or will benefit by it, is no more an act of benevolence than is throwing down a handful of coppers to be scrambled for in the street.

Another of the most dangerous and difficult sort of benevolent people are those who are always willing to do everything for everybody, who go about with a long string of *protégés* whom they are ready to foist upon us on the smallest excuse. These general accepters and protectors of waifs and strays are very troublesome folk. In the first place, because so evenly is desert and deserving apportioned, even in this life, that I believe few people remain waifs and strays permanently, without there being some inherent cause for that condition. Trouble comes alike to all ; but some deserve it — others do not. Some rise out of it—have the faculty to rise out of it ; others never rise, and apparently have no care or wish to rise. And your carelessly benevolent people refuse to draw the distinction. Even if you draw it for them, they meet you with an avalanche of texts, such as, "He maketh his sun to shine upon the just and the unjust," &c., &c.

They forget that they are not Providence. Besides, according to them, their *protégés* are never bad, only unfortunate. Their geese are always swans—in their eyes, simply because they patronise them. Patronage is so pleasant, and to be followed by a little crowd of admirers is so soothing to the benevolent mind. So they annoy us unbenevolent people at their pleasure, by supplying the best of characters to incompetent servants, offering as candidates for important situations persons who have no recommendation whatever for the position, except the need of it, and so on. These are they who entreat us to get published feeble MSS., on the feebler plea that the authors "wish to add a little to their income," or have experienced reverses, or would like to earn something for a benevolent purpose. As if these were any reasons for trying to do what they cannot do, or for others aiding them therein; since, as a rule, good work deserves good pay, and will get it; bad work should get nothing, however great the need of the doer of it.

But our short-sighted, kindly meaning friends cannot see this. They still keep urging us to employ unsuitable servants, who want our place so badly; to send our children to a particular school, or to deal at some special shop, not because it is the best school or the best shop, but because "the poor things are so ill off, you see; it is quite a charity."

Why are they so ill off? Is there not a cause

for it? Accidental misfortune will happen to all; but, as I have said, and the observation of life forces me to believe it more firmly every year, no one ever remains unfortunate, without there being, generally speaking, some recondite reason, some "screw loose" somewhere, accounting for the fact. It may be a hard saying, but I fear it is only too true, that nobody ever becomes a permanent "object of charity," without having ceased to deserve it.

This rule especially applies to the large class of which all of us know so many, who are said to live "from hand to mouth," the mouth being usually their own, and the hand that of their friends; or rather the acquaintances who successively acquire and renounce the title.

> " Neither a borrower nor a lender be,
> For debt oft loses both itself and friend."

Itself, because the borrower seldom becomes such till he is in circumstances which make repayment at least doubtful; the friend, because two friends who have been placed in that position together rarely recover the old relation entirely. A gift, out and out, is often a real

pleasure, an exceeding boon; but a loan, if ever
repaid, or very long of repayment, always places
both parties in a false position. There is a sense
of humiliation on the one side, of being made
use of on the other, which creates reserve at any
rate, even between sincere friends; and, if there
has been in the transaction the slightest insincerity, is fatal in its results. You pity, you
pardon; you regret, you apologize; but you two
are never quite as you were before. Of course
there is no rule without exceptions; still, ordinarily speaking, they are the wisest people who
follow Polonius's advice, and as long as possible
preserve themselves from being either borrowers
or lenders.

But there is a form of borrowing and lending
which becomes, on both sides, an error so great
as to be little short of an actual crime : in the
borrower, who borrows without hope or intention of repayment; in the lender, who does
what he is asked to do from no sense of kindness, or justice, or even charity, but just "to get
rid of the fellow," or from being himself "a
fellow that can't say No." Worse sometimes,

a fellow who, from some business or worldly reason concerning the borrower and himself, is afraid of the consequences of saying No. Therefore he allows himself to pay a sort of black mail to the unworthy levier thereof; hating and grudging, but still paying it, and flattering himself that it looks like benevolence.

The cowardice of such conduct is only equalled by its folly. If my friend, so called, writes to me again and again, " Lend me five pounds to save me from ruin," the only rational reply is, " If only five pounds stands between you and ruin, you had better be ruined, and have done with it." To be perpetually stopping up a hole, which yawns the next day wider than ever, is the act not of generosity but of stupidity. Many a man has gone to ruin, the real ruin he first made a pretence of, because some weak, foolish relative or friend to whom he applied for money had not the sense to refuse it at once ; absolutely, remorselessly, at all cost of pain and wounded feeling between himself and his would-be debtor. Better a passing coolness than an enmity for life.

They who, for any of the motives here named—motives, you will observe, which affect their own personality more than the borrower's—continue lending to unfortunate people, simply because they are unfortunate, are guilty on three counts: first, towards themselves, for a pretence of generosity which is only egotistic selfishness; secondly, towards the person they attempt to benefit, whom they do not benefit but rather injure; thirdly, towards other and worthier persons, whom they lose the power of helping, by having helped unworthy ones.

For the really deserving neither beg nor borrow—they suffer silently; while the loud-complaining, ever-greedy applicants for aid, always get the best of what charity is going. I often think that much of the benevolence in this world is poured out like pig-wash: the pig who makes most noise, or who succeeds in getting his two feet in the trough while the others have but one, is the animal who swallows most and fattens fastest.

That before-mentioned sixpence thrown to a mendicant, only to be converted into gin or beer, that five pounds lent to a needy acquaintance, who always has been needy and always will be, because he has not the slightest sense of the value of money, nor the least conscience in obtaining it, or spending it,—these, with a hundred similar cases, are specimens of what I call the crime of benevolence. The donors err, not only in what they do, but in what they leave undone. They may be benevolent in vague intention, but of true beneficence they have not the slightest idea.

The difference is this. Benevolence consists in mere kind feeling ; doing good certainly sometimes, but in a vague and careless way, and more for its own pleasure than for another's benefit; giving, because to give is agreeable, but taking little pains to ascertain what has been the result of the gift. The donor has done his part, and that is enough. It may be another heresy, but I am afraid the reason that our charitable institutions are so numerous, and our subscription lists so easy to fill up, is because, of all modes of benevolence, giving of money is the one which involves least trouble.

But beneficence does cost trouble. It requires in the individual some rather rare qualities; powers of administration and patient investigation; clear judgment and capacity for work; a kind heart, and a cool head, ay, and a hard head, too. The power of saying No, and the will to say it, with a steady, strong, unvarying justice, are as necessary as quick sympathy and ready help.

Though, in the main, true beneficence aims less at helping people than at enabling them to help themselves, there will always be in the world a large amount of those who cannot possibly help themselves : the sick, the aged, the young, the hopelessly feeble and incapable. It is the more necessary that anybody who can do anything should be left to do it, or taught to do it, for Beneficence is always more of a teacher than a preacher. She would be more prone to set up a cookery-school than a soup-kitchen; and would consider the building of a row of workmen's cottages, well arranged, well drained, well ventilated, of rather more importance than the erection of the finest church imaginable.

I think it is an open question how far real
beneficence has to do with charity, *i.e.* giving
of money, at all. Secondarily, of course, it must,
but primarily. I was once talking with a lady
whose name is sufficiently well known, though I
will not give it here, and who has done more
good in ameliorating the condition of the London
poor than all the philanthropists, religious and
otherwise, who have flooded the metropolis with
their bounty, and left it, people say, especially
at the East end, rather worse than they found
it, in a condition of expectant pauperism, which
is for ever crying, " Give, give, give." Now,
this lady told me, that during all the years of
her dealings with the poor—the very poor—
whom she has slowly lifted from the condition of
savages, the savagery of London courts and
alleys, into intelligent human beings—during
all these years, she said, she had never given, in
mere charity, one single shilling. Fair pay-
ment for fair work, was the principle she in-
variably went upon. She planned houses,
with every comfort that a working man's
family could require, but she exacted from her

tenants the weekly rent, and when they did not pay she turned them out; she found employment for all that would do it, but if not done it was not paid for; she assisted the women in their efforts to become good housewives, taught them to cook, to sew, to make clothes; she went from house to house, leaving behind her plenty of good advice and kindly sympathy, but never either a tract or a half-penny. She took endless trouble, ran no end of risks, and exerted an influence, almost miraculous, over her rough community; but from first to last, she said, her experience was this, " Help the poor to help themselves. Give them advice, instruction, work —mixed with plenty of sympathy. Sometimes, in very hard cases, money's worth, such as clothes or food, but never under any circumstances give them money."

Yet this lady is one of the very few philanthropists who have really met their reward, and seen the work of their hands prosper. Her little kingdom, which she rules with a kindly though most firm hand, is full of subjects who not only obey but love her. She enters fear-lessly into courts and alleys of the lowest class, known hitherto only to the inspector of nuisances and the police detective; she commences her reforms, and by-and-by the wild inhabitants are found as decent folk, living in decent dwellings, amenable to law, common sense, and kindly feeling.

Moreover, she succeeds in what almost all charities fail in—she actually makes it pay. She has gained a small per-centage on the money employed, of which she has been so long the wise administrator. And this fact is confirmatory of another axiom of hers, proved by her own experience, that no charity effects so much permanent good as one which is, or soon can be made, self-supporting. In short, such is the necessary mutual relation between the helped and the helpers, the poor and the rich, that the former cease to value what they can get for nothing, and the latter soon find that while they think they are assisting the poor, they are only sinking them from honest independence to weak dependence, from mere poverty into absolute pauperdom.

I cannot more clearly describe what I mean by benevolence and beneficence than by putting this lady's work—the work of a lifetime—side by side with that in the "charitable" parish I have mentioned—also anonymously—where money was poured out like water, and the needy had but to ask and to have. Here, on the contrary, nothing was done from charity, everything from justice: the common justice between man and man which makes the labourer worthy of his hire, the rentpayer deserving of a decent house to live in—as good a house of its kind for a mechanic as for a gentleman; but at the same time exacting from the poor man, in proportion to his means, precisely the same honesty, sobriety, and conscientiousness that is exacted in the class above him.

Until "gentlefolk" believe this, and cease to regard their servants, clerks, &c., as inferior beings, from whom nothing is to be expected but a hand-to-hand struggle between rich and poor, employer and employed, as to who shall have the best of it; until they give up the system of treating their dependants as mere machines, out of whom as much work is to be got as possible; or as brute beasts, for whom no training answers but whipping or feeding, and to whom they may throw their charity as they would throw a bone at a dog, with as little care for the result of it;—until this state of things ends, there must be always that secret enmity between class and class, that half-concealed, half-acknowledged difference in morals, feelings, and principles, which constitute the main difficulty of those who would fain have but one law of right for all, and look upon every man who fulfilled it as "a man and a brother."

There is another phase of the crime of benevolence, unconnected with money, which ought not to be passed over; that is the leniency with which some very well disposed people get to look on moral turpitude. Some do it through mere laziness or indifference. "It is not my business; why should I give myself any trouble about it?" So they shut their eyes to wickedness—in their rich neighbour, whom they ask to dinner, though they are not quite sure he was too honest in that business transaction of last week; in their poor domestic, say, their coachman, who they know gets drunk every Saturday night, and beats his wife; but the lodge is too far off to hear her cries, and, the carriage not being out of Sundays, John cannot drive his master into a ditch. So, since John is a good servant, and knows his business well, the master ignores the whole matter of the drunkenness: to notice it would be so very inconvenient. And Mr. Blank, whose acquaintance it would be so awkward to give up, is smiled upon blandly; until some day he happens to be taken up for forgery.

Others take their stand upon the divine saying, " I came not to call the righteous but sinners to repentance;" and obeying it in their imperfect, finite way, gradually cease to take interest in any except sinners. All the drunkards of the parish, the unwived mothers, the scapegrace children, come to them, and by canting phrases of oft-repeated contrition, and voluble promises of never-fulfilled amendment, coax them out of the benefits that honest people

never get. The greater the sinner the greater
the saint is, either really or ostensibly, their
permanent creed. They take up with all the
scamps in the parish, while the respectable
working man—thank heaven, there is still many
a one in our England, as honourable as any
working gentleman, and often as true a gentleman at heart!—has with them no chance
at all.

True, these so-called Christians have always
plenty of arguments on their side; especially
the parable of the Prodigal Son, and the "joy
in heaven over one sinner that repenteth." But
they forget that the prodigal when his father
met him was no longer a prodigal; he had
forsaken his evil ways, never to return to them
more. Also, that the "joy" is supposed to be
over a repentant sinner, not a sinner who still
remains in sin. Christ, in His divinest charity,
never does more for offenders than to pardon
them, until they cease to offend. "Go," He
says; "go and sin no more, lest a worse thing
happen unto thee." But for those who continue
to sin there is, even according to the quoters of

Holy Writ—often so egregiously twisted and misapplied—a worse thing ; even as in the parable of the fig-tree : "Cut it down ; why cumbereth it the ground ?" And sometimes the kindest, wisest, most Christian act is—to let it be cut down.

For instance, every one who gives money to a confirmed drunkard or profligate, thereby encouraging him in his vices ; every one who, for any reason, however compassionate, speaks what is called "a good word" for a person whom he knows to be bad, condones sin, and is guilty of the result that follows. His lazy laxity allows these cumberers of the ground to take the life from wholesome trees. And, even as a man who sits with his hands folded, and allows his humble neighbours to wallow in dirt like pigs, saying, "I can't help it; it is not my affair," may one day have to see ghastly fever, bred in those backslums, stalk in at his own front door, and carry off his best-beloved child ; so any one who laughs at error as mere "folly," and puts a plaister upon ugly sin, connives dangerously at both.

M

He has shirked what was unpleasant; he has been too lazy to take trouble; he has done his benevolence in the easiest way. He may yet have to pay for his mistaken mercy by being ground under the ever-moving wheel of an unerring justice; justice which, though it does not always reward, assuredly knows the way to punish.

He is punished, this pseudo-benevolent person. He is eaten up by grasping, needy, ravenous dependants. He has often to stand helplessly by, and watch the widening spread of evils, which he might have stopped at once if he had only had the courage to take hold of vice and slay it with a strong, firm hand. He thinks himself bitterly wronged, and accuses the world of shameful ingratitude : it does not strike him that the world really owes him nothing, since what he did was done to please himself.

This especially applies to certain people, who for a time may gain much outside credit, which is indeed the thing they most desire,—those who delight in what they call "magnificence."

They it is who always give a cabman half-a-crown when a shilling is his right fare; who distribute money right and left in gratuities to servants; who always make the handsomest of presents (especially to their rich friends), and like to head every subscription-list far above the rest. They never think that the cabman they over-pay will grumble at the next person who pays him his right fare, and no more; that nothing so degrades, or even offends a good servant as to be requited in money for a simple kindness; that the worth of a gift is nothing—the spirit of it everything; and that to see your neighbour's name down in a charity-list for a larger sum than either he or you can afford, is much more apt to make you close your purse-strings than to open them.

Your "magnificent" people are in some things worse than the merely lavish, who give recklessly of that which costs them nothing; they give deliberately, for the mere credit of giving, and for their own glorification. The praise of men is mostly their sole aim. That "cup of cold water" which the Divine Master named so tenderly, would be a drink quite too mean, too discreditable (to themselves), to offer unto anybody. It must be the best of wine, in a jewelled goblet, or must not be offered at all.

Their notions of a present, too (and they give a good many of them), is the handsomest thing that money can purchase. A much handsomer thing than anybody else has given, and something that will make people cry out, "Whose gift is that? What a very generous person he must be!" But the suitableness of the present, and whether the recipient needed it or wished for it, is quite another thing. And unless the said recipient, whether pleased or not, pretends to be so, and overwhelms him with gratitude and delight, our "magnificent" friend is exceedingly offended.

Speaking of this matter of giving presents, it is curious how few know how to bestow or to accept one, whether it be a kindly benefaction, from him who does not need to him who does, or a *cadeau* as the French term it, in their nice distinction of language—a "keepsake" between two people who are equals, if not friends.

I remember being much astonished (it was in the simple days of youth, when a good deal astonished one that does not astonish now), by hearing a conversation between a husband and wife, who had just received a present from a near relative whom they did not very much care for. They criticized it, they found fault with it; they speculated as to what was the person's intention in sending it, and what was to be sent back in return.

"Of course we must send something, and immediately," said the gentleman, who was of the "magnificent" order; "I wish we could find out exactly what it cost, and then we could give them back one worth as much and a little over." "Just as much will do, I think, my dear," added the wife, who, like most wives of "magnificent" men, was obliged to think of economy. "But we must give something; they will expect it."

This expecting something in return for a present is surely one of the meanest of feelings; yet it is at the root of half the gifts given. Marriage, christening, birthday presents are made, not because people wish to give, but because they think they ought, and that other people will expect it of them. Gifts irksome to receive, and sometimes actually wrong to offer, as either draining purses already too slender, or irritating those who can afford it by a kind of feeling that, as everybody knows they can afford it, they must give more than anybody else. If the "happy pair" who exhibit a roomful of such offerings could know all that they subject their friends to, or their friends foolishly subject themselves to, in this matter, they would turn with disgust from most of the presents they receive. I am not sure that it is not the truest kindness as well as wisdom to say point-blank, "I never give anything to anybody."

Yet a gift is a pleasant thing, rightly given; most pleasant and dear and sacred, whether its value be much or little, if only it is offered with the heart, and chosen from the heart. Chosen with care and pains, and a tender anxiety that it should be exactly the thing we liked and wanted. It is so sweet to be remembered and taken trouble over, even in the smallest things. But gifts carelessly given—merely to gratify a love of giving, which some people have even to a disease—given without thought of whether they will be useful or not, whether the receiver will care for them or not, are, between friends, often a great vexation; between strangers, or any who are not exactly equals, a burden of obligation simply intolerable.

The child, with its innocent sudden kiss, and its earnest, "Thank you so much!" for a doll's sash, or a penny toy, which it really wanted, comes much nearer the true theory of giving and receiving than hundreds of people who weary themselves in choosing handsome presents, or in returning equivalents for the same— presents which, the instant after they are made, become, like stopped cheques, "of no value to anybody," not even to the possessor.

These—like the charity which is indifferent to error, and ready to overlook every sin that is not personally inconvenient to itself, as well as the generosity which looks not to the advantage of its object, but its own—these three may all go under the head of that sort of benevolence which, if not an actual crime, is a very great mistake and an egregious folly.

Why?

Here, again, we come to the root of things. Why? Because it is content with wishing well, instead of doing well. Because whatever good it does is done, not for duty's sake, for righteousness' sake, for God's sake, but merely for its own sake; to gratify its vanity, to ease its conscience, to heal up its wounded self-esteem with the smooth cataplasm of gratitude.

But true beneficence never looks for gratitude at all. What it does is not done with a view to itself, but solely for the sake of that other whom it desires to benefit; and above all for His sake who is the source of all charity. There is a deep truth in the passionate pleading of the Irish beggar: "Shure, sir, ye'll do it; not for the love o' me—for the love o' God." Therefore real beneficence, which does all its good deeds for the love of God, is neither vainglorious nor exacting; not easily wounded, and never offended. It goes straight on, doing what it believes to be right and best, without any reference to what people may say of it, and whether the recipients of its bounty are grateful or not.

A word about gratitude, which some people seem to think the natural result and reward of benevolence—to follow as unerringly as day follows night. Alas! they had much better say as night follows day; for kindly deeds as often end in darkness as in light—at least what seems like darkness to our human eyes. Unless benevolence, like virtue, can be its own reward, it must often rest satisfied with no reward at all.

What matter? Of course, gratitude is a welcome thing; in this weary world a most refreshing thing; but it is not an indispensable thing. It warms the heart and cheers the spirit, but it has nothing to do with either benevolence or beneficence, nor is it the origin or end of either. The wisest people are they, who, though happy to get thanks, never expect them, and can do without them. Such may be deceived and disappointed, but they are never embittered; because their motive lay deeper, and is higher, than anything belonging to this world. The truly benevolent man is he who, looking on all his charities great or small, says only—in devout repetition of his Master's words—"I have finished the work which Thou gavest me to do," —not that which I gave myself to do, and not that which I did for myself, but that which Thou gavest me and I have done for Thee. To such the answer comes, even as in Lowell's touching ballad of "Sir Launfal:"

> " The Holy Supper is kept indeed
> In what we share with another's need;
> Not what we give, but what we share,
> For the gift without the giver is bare;
> Who gives himself with his alms, feeds three:
> Himself—his hungering neighbour—and ME."

Sermon V.

MY BROTHER'S KEEPER.

V.

MY BROTHER'S KEEPER.

ARE we, or are we not—our brother's keeper? That is, to what extent are we responsible for those beneath us, or dependent upon us, or connected with us by any link which gives us power with regard to them or influence over them?

This is, I think, the point at issue between those who are called philanthropists, and those others—well, I suppose no one would voluntarily dub himself misanthropist—but those who refuse to "bother" themselves with their brother's affairs; to whom the question, "Who is my neighbour?" is as indifferent as the naturally succeeding one, "What have I to do for him?" —in fact, people who, though they would be much offended if you said so, are of the

same type as the most respectable priest and
Levite who preceded the good Samaritan in
passing by him who "fell among thieves."

A parable often misapplied, since many of
the way-laid sufferers for whom our sympathy is
demanded are very often thieves themselves;
the weak, the selfish, the unprincipled; who live
by robbing honest people, and by laying on
others the burden of their self-created woes.
But it is not of them I have now to speak, but
of those designated by the word " brother."

In the first place, who is our brother ?

There are those who will tell us it is the
negro, the South-Sea Islander—the " heathen
Chinee;" whom, as the first of moral duties,
we must try to convert—(of course, to our own
special form of Christianity, any other being
worse than none, which a little complicates
matters). Nevertheless, it must be done. And
conversion gained, all else will follow.

Be it so. Let those go proselyting who feel
themselves thereto called. There is work
enough in the world for all; innumerable
" brothers "—and very few who are fit, in any

sense, to be their "keepers." But let not this interesting black or brown brother far away shut out from our sight the white brother who stands at our very door. Stand, did I say?—He crawls—he grovels—not only outside but actually within our doors. We can scarcely take a step without treading upon him—even though we may shut our eyes to the sight of him.

And we do shut our eyes, either intentionally or unintentionally. We prefer looking a long way off—upon objects picturesque and heroic. The "noble savage" running wild in his "native woods" is a much more interesting subject of civilisation than Billy the washerwoman's boy, especially when entering our family as William the boy in buttons. Yet, perhaps, he no less needs the care, and could be developed into at least as good a Christian, and at a somewhat cheaper rate. And the feminine hearts who yearn over the "condition of women in India" would find as worthy an object for their reformatory sympathy in Jane the gardener's wife, with six children, living in two rooms upon a pound a week,—or Emma the housemaid, insanely spending all her large wages upon dress, and leaving herself not a half-penny for sickness or old age.

"Charity begins at home"—the old-fashioned proverb used to say. But the peculiarity of our large-minded modern society is that "home" either does not exist, or that it is the last place in the world about which charity ever troubles itself.

I have been led to this train of thought by two articles which appeared lately in a well-known Magazine, on the much-vexed question of domestic servants. The writers took opposite sides : one defended the lower class against the upper ; protested against the extreme ill-usage sustained by servants in general, and contended for their "privileges," averring that they ought to be allowed full time to cultivate their intellects—and that among other refinements there should be a library in every pantry, and a pianoforte in every kitchen. The opposing paper took the mistresses' side—the much-tried, much-enduring mistresses ; and, so far from allowing our domestics any rights would fain

have reduced servitude to its original meaning, and considered servants somewhat as the
ancients considered their slaves—an altogether
different order of beings from themselves. The
first protested loudly that we were all brothers;
though the great point—which of us was to be
"our brother's keeper"—was left untouched.
The second, so far as I remember, almost denied
that there was a common human nature between
the kitchen and the parlour.

Both meant well, I verily believe; and both
had a certain justice in their arguments. But
the real truth, as in most contests, lay between
the two. Let us consider it a little.

Few will deny the melancholy fact that the
servant question is growing more difficult year
by year. Perhaps, naturally so, since every
class is rising and trying to force itself into the
class above it—a not ignoble aim, if it at the
same time educates and fits itself to enter that
class; but it mostly does not do this. Therefore,
a continual struggle goes on—a continual push-
ing up of heterogeneous elements into the
already wildly seething mass—and the result is

—chaos? Let us hope not. Let us trust that all will settle in time. Providence knows its own business much better than we do.

Still we must do our business, too, and do it our very best. Anything short of our best is setting ourselves in opposition—oh, how futile! —to Providence, and consequently to our own selves. He only who works with God, so far as he sees, works for God, and for himself at the same time.

Those who remember the servants of even twenty-five years ago cannot fail to discover a great change in the whole class—as a class. Far less work is done by each individual; and far more wages expected. The most faithful, intelligent, and clever servant I ever knew began life at thirteen years old, as maid-of-all-work in the family of a gentleman—a poor one certainly, still it was "a gentleman's family," —consisting of himself, his wife, and three children. Her wages the first year were three pounds per annum. What would be thought of such a "place" nowadays? Yet it turned out not a bad one. The girl was taken literally as "one of the family." The mistress trained her; the little ones loved her; the eldest daughter educated her—ay, up to a point that even the aforesaid article would approve, for she could read and understand Shakspere, and write as good a letter as most young ladies when they leave school and marry. She never married, but she remained faithful to the family in weal and woe—far more woe than weal, alas!—until she died, but not until she had served two generations. Her grave has been green now for many a year, yet the last remnant of that family never hears the sound of her name—a very common one, "Bessy"—without a throb of remembrance too sweet for tears.

This is what servants used to be, as many an old family tradition will prove. What are they now?

As an answer I could put forward two illustrative anecdotes; of the butler who threw up his place because he had "always been accustomed to have a sofa in his pantry," and the parlour-maid who, having accepted a situation, declined to go because she and her luggage were to be fetched from the station in a spring-cart, whereas in her last place they had sent the carriage and a footman to meet her. These are, I hope, exceptional instances, but we all know what our own and our friends' servants are, in the main.

As to dress, for instance. If extravagant folly of toilette were not becoming so common in all ranks, we should be absolutely startled by the attire of our cooks and parlour-maids—on Sundays especially. And it is so utterly out of proportion to their means. Fancy our grandmothers giving Jenny the housemaid to Thomas the gardener to settle down in holy matrimony upon —say a pound a week; and they are seen walking to church—he in a fine black suit, and she in a light silk gown, tulle bonnet and veil, and a wreath of orange blossom! Yet such has been the costume at more than one wedding which has lately come under my notice; and I believe it is the usual style of such, in that class.

Then as to eating and drinking; the extent to which this goes on in large and wealthy families is something incredible. Stout footmen, dainty ladies' maids, and under servants of all kinds expect to be fed with the fat of the land, and to drink in proportion. It is not enough to say that they live as well as their masters and mistresses—they often live much better; the kind of fare that satisfied twenty or forty years ago would be intolerable now. Expense and waste they never think of; they are only comers and goers according to their own convenience, and the more they get out of their "places" during their temporary stay the better.

This, too, is another sad change. A house where the servants remain is becoming such an exception as to be quite notable in the neighbourhood.

"Why did I come after your place, ma'am?" answered a decent elderly man, applying for a situation as gardener. "To tell you the truth, I heard yours was a place where the servants stayed; so I thought it would suit me, and my wife too, and I came after it." Of course, he was taken, and will probably end his days there.

But most servants are rolling stones which

gather no moss. Nor wish it even; they prefer moving about. They change their mistresses as easily as their caps. The idea of considering themselves as members of the family—to stick to it, as it to them, through all difficulties not absolutely overwhelming—would be held as simply ridiculous. To them "master" is merely the man who pays; and "missis," the woman who "worrits." That between these and themselves there could be any common interest, or deep sympathy of any kind, never enters their imagination. Nor, alas! does it into that of the upper half of the household. If the mistress, with a child dangerously ill up-stairs, is shocked to hear the unchecked merriment in the servants' hall, why does she forget that not long ago she refused to let her cook away to see a dying sister because of that day's dinner-party? "It would have been so very inconvenient, you know. Afterwards, I let her go immediately." Yes, but—the sister was dead.

This may be a sharply drawn picture, but I ask, is it overdrawn? Is it not the average state of the relation nowadays between masters and servants?

There may be strict uprightness, liberality, even kindness on the one side, and duty satisfactorily done on the other; but of sympathy—the common human bond between man and man, or woman and woman—there is almost none. Nobody gives it, and nobody expects to find it.

Why is this? Or can it be the reason—there must be a reason—that everybody declares it is almost impossible to get good servants?

May I suggest that perhaps this may arise from the fact of servants finding it so exceedingly difficult to get good masters and mistresses?

By good I mean not merely good-natured, well-meaning people, but those who have a deeply rooted conscientious sense of responsibility—who believe themselves to be, as superiors, constituted by God, not merely the rulers, but the guide and guard of their inferiors; and whose life is spent in finding out the best way in which that solemn duty can be fulfilled.

In every age, evil as well as good takes root downwards and bears fruit upwards. All reformations, as well as all corruptions, begin

with the upper class and descend to the lower.
Even as there is seldom an irredeemable naughty
child without the parents being in some way to
blame, so we rarely hear of a household tormented by a long succession of bad servants
without suspecting that possibly the master and
mistress may not be altogether such innocent
victims as they imagine themselves.

For it is from them, the heads of the house,
that the house necessarily takes its tone. If a
lady spends a large proportion of her income on
milliners and dressmakers, how can she issue
sumptuary laws to her cook and housemaid? If
a gentleman habitually consumes as much wine
as he can safely drink—perhaps a little more,
though he is never so ungenteel as actually to
get "drunk"—how can he blame John the coachman, or William the gardener, that they do get
drunk—they who have nothing else to amuse
themselves with? For their master takes no
care to supply anything that they rationally
can amuse themselves with, being as indifferent
to their minds as he is to their bodies. So that
both are kept going like machinery, ready to do

their necessary work, nothing else is needed,
and nothing ever inquired into. They, the
master and mistress, are not their "brother's"
keepers,—they are only his employers. They
use him, criticize him, control him, are even
kind to him in a sort of way, but they have no
sympathy with him whatever.

This is apparently the weak point—the small
wheel broken—which produces most of the jar-
ring in the present machinery of society. The
tie between upper and lower classes has become loosened—has sunk into a mere matter
of convenience. Not that the superior is intentionally unkind ; in fact, he bestows on his
inferiors many a benefit ; but he does not give
it, or exchange it ; he throws it at him much
as you would throw a bone at a dog, with the
quiet conviction, "Take it—it is for your good ;
but you are the dog, and I am the man, for all
that."

Is this right—or necessary ? That there
should be distinctions of classes is necessary.
Rich and poor, masters and servants, must
always exist ; but need they be pitted against

each other—the one ruling, the other resisting; the one exacting, the other denying, to the utmost of their mutual power? That mysterious link, which can bind together the most opposite elements, and which, in default of a better term, I have called sympathy—though using it more in the French than English meaning of the word—is altogether wanting.

Was it always so? In olden times, when the primitive institution of rude slavery softened into feudal servitude—the weak hiding together under shelter of the strong, and the ignorant putting themselves under the guidance of the educated—undoubtedly the relation was very different. The line of division between class and class was drawn as distinctly as now, and yet the bond was much closer and tenderer. The feudal lord had his retainers, the lady her serving-maids. These she instructed in all domestic duties, even as he trained his men in the field. The root of the relationship was, of course, mutual advantage; but it blossomed into mutual kindliness, and bore fruit in that fidelity which is not lessened but increased by the consciousness of mutual dependence. The difference of rank was, so far as we can discover, maintained in these old days as strongly as now; but it was like the difference between parent and child—where the one exercises, and the other submits to, an authority which is not mere arbitrary rule, but wise control and generous protection.

This, I think, is the point which all shoot wide of nowadays; the magic charm which nobody can find. They will not recognise that the kingly relation—for every head of a household must be a king therein, nay, an autocrat, since a wise autocracy is the safest and simplest form of government—the regal relation also includes the parental. The Romans understood this in the words " paterfamilias," " materfamilias; " "familias" implying not only the children but the servants. Is it too startling a theory to assert that the heads of a large household are nearly as responsible for their servants as they are for their children? and that the servants owe them the same kind of duty—faithfulness, gratitude, loving obedience?

Not blind obedience, but a clear-sighted submission; which must be won, not compelled;
and can only be won by the exercise of those
qualities—the only qualities which justify one
human being in being the master of another.
This, I believe, is the principle upon which
we are constituted "our brother's keeper."
A principle which modern masters and mistresses, who take their servants from the nearest
register office, and return them thence when
they have done with them, will call perfectly
Utopian. Did they ever try to put it in
practice?

In the first place, what is their definition of
a servant? A person who will do the pre-
scribed work in the most satisfactory manner,
for reasonable wages, and, beyond that, give
as little trouble as possible. Somebody who
comes when convenient, is treated as convenient, and got rid of also when convenient,
to the establishment. If servants "suit" the
place, or the place suits them, they stay; if not,
they go; and there is an end of it. The idea
that they "enter a family," as the phrase is,

to become from that day an integral portion of it, to share its joys and sorrows, labours and cares, and to receive from it a corresponding amount of interest and sympathy, thereby commencing and cementing a permanent tie not to be broken except by serious misconduct or misfortune, or any of those inevitables which no one can guard against—this old-fashioned notion never occurs to anybody.

Hence the rashness with which such engagements are formed. The carelessness manifested by most people in engaging their servants is almost inconceivable. The "place" is applied for; or the mistress applies at a register office. Out of numerous candidates she selects those she thinks most likely; the "character" is sought and supplied; if that is satisfactory, all is settled; and a man or woman, whom nobody knows anything of, is thereupon brought into the family, to hold in it the most intimate relation possible. Of course, such an arrangement may succeed; but the chances that it will not succeed are enormous.

This formality of " getting a character" has often seemed to me one of the most curious delusions that sensible people labour under. When written it is almost valueless ; anybody can forge it, or, even giving it *bonâ fide,* may express it in such a way as to convey anything but the real truth. Besides, is that truth the real truth ? When we consider the prejudices, the vexations, on both sides, which often arise in parting with a servant, can we always depend upon a faithful statement, or upon those who make it ? I have often thought that, instead of inquiring any servant's character, we ought rather to inquire the character of the late mistress.

Besides, as a rule, a really efficient servant needs no character at all. Such a one on leaving a situation is sure to have half-a-dozen families eager to secure so rare and valuable a possession. A good servant never lacks a place ; a good master or mistress rarely finds any want of good servants. Temporary difficulties may befall both ; but in the long run it is thus. Even as—if one carefully notices the course of the world—every man, be he religious or irreligious, will come, at the middle or end of life, to the same conclusion as David :—" I have been young, and now am old; yet *never* saw I the righteous forsaken, nor his seed begging their bread." Not that all is smooth, or easy, or fortunate ; on the contrary, " Many are the troubles of the righteous ;" but " the Lord delivereth him out of them all."

And so, to measure small things by great, I believe that, though accidental difficulties may arise, a good servant may drift into a bad place, a conscientious master or mistress may be cheated here and there by unfaithful servants, still, in the long run, things right themselves. No law is more certain in its ultimate working than that which affirms that all people find their own level, and reap their own deservings.

But to come to practicalities—and yet I believe no practical work is ever done so well as when it has a strong spiritual sense at the core of it— what is the first thing to be considered in choosing one's servants ? I answer, unhesitatingly—their moral nature.

"What!" I hear some fashionable mistress exclaim, "trouble myself about the moral nature of John the footman, or Sarah the cook —or even, though they come closer in contact with me, of my housemaid, nurse, or lady's maid? Impossible! simply ridiculous! So that they do their work well, and don't trouble me, that is all I require."

Is it all? You are then content to have about you continually mere machines, the motive power of whose existence you are utterly ignorant of? What hold have you upon them? what guard against them? what guarantee for virtue, or preservative from vice? Vice which, say what you like, must affect you and yours, sometimes in the very closest way.

Nothing is more remarkable than the extreme foolhardiness, to say the least of it, with which respectable families put themselves at the mercy of strange servants, of whose antecedents they know nothing, or know only that they are capable of doing their allotted work, are "trained parlour-maids," "good plain cooks," and so on. But of their moral characteristics, their tempers, principles, habits—all that constitutes the difference between bad people and good, those who are a comfort and help, or else an absolute torment and curse in a household, the heads of that household are in entire ignorance. Yet they expect, besides efficiency in work, all the fidelity, conscientiousness, and other good qualities which they would have found in a person whom they had known all their lives, who was trained in all their ways, and accustomed to all their peculiarities.

Do they never consider that in this, as in most things, we only get what we earn, and can get nothing without earning it? That if we want really good servants, we must make them such? We must bring them up, even as we bring up our children, with the same care and patience, making allowance for the nice distinctions of character in every human being; and, above all, having the same sense of responsibility, though in a lesser degree, that we have concerning our own family.

To this end it is advisable to take young

servants, which most people object to. They prefer domestics ready made, that is, made by other people, who have had all the trouble of training them. But these can never suit us so well, or have the same personal attachment for us, as those we have trained ourselves.

For I hold—strange doctrine nowadays!— that personal attachment is the real pivot upon which all domestic service turns. It may sound very ridiculous that a lady should try to win the hearts of her cooks and housemaids, and a gentleman trouble himself as to whether his coachman or gardener had a respectful regard for "master." Yet otherwise little real good is effected on either side.

Without love, all service becomes mere eye-service, or at best a cold matter-of-fact doing one's duty: any attempts at training are almost useless; and with already trained and efficient servants, their very efficiency is, the heart being wanting, an unsatisfactory thing, —like being served by the two hands, which waited upon the Prince in the fairy tale of the White Cat. Admirably competent hands, no doubt, but a poor exchange for the bright face and pleasant voice of what children call "a person," and a person that loves us.

I am bold enough to say that, in a really happy and well-arranged houshould, it is absolutely indispensable that the servants should really love "the family," and be loved by them. Under no other conditions can the duty which is laid upon us of being our brother's keeper be thoroughly fulfilled. And how is this to be done?

"I can't imagine why it is that my servants never take to me," said a very kind but reserved mistress, complaining to another who was more happily circumstanced; "I am sure I mean them well—would do all I could for them, only somehow I never know how to talk to them."

That is the very reason. Most people never talk to their servants at all. They "speak" to them with patronising benignity, they order them, find fault with them, or sharply scold them; but anything beyond that, anything that brings the two human beings face to face as human beings, such as cordial praise for well-doing; quiet, serious, sorrowful rebuke for ill-doing; sympathy in trouble; and last, not least, an equally quick sympathy in their pleasures and amusements — is a thing unthought of on either side. Class and class go on their parallel lines, close together, yet eternally apart.

It is sad as strange sometimes to notice the way in which presumably good people speak to servants, either with a cold, repellent reserve, or a furious unreserve, such as they would never use towards any other. Now he who flies into a rage and insults an equal may be a fool, but he who insults an inferior is worse—he is a coward. Many a gentleman in his stable, and many a lady in her kitchen or nursery, would do well to pause before condemning themselves as such.

Nevertheless, to "spoil" a servant is as dangerous as spoiling a child. In both cases, discipline must be kept up. The head of a household is justified in laying down for it the strictest laws, and insisting that they shall not be broken. Mistresses might with advantage be very much severer than many now take the trouble to be, against waste, over-dressing, over-feeding ; perquisites, visitors, and all the luxurious items which make servants so expensive — to the family's injury and their own. And, laws once laid down, no alternative must be accepted. "Obey, or you leave my service," is the only safe rule.

But this strictness is compatible with the utmost kindliness, nay, even familiarity. A mistress who is sure of her own position, and safely entrenched in her own quiet dignity, may be almost a mother to her servants without fearing from them the slightest over-familiarity. Nay, she will not lose their respect by actually helping in their work, or at least showing them that she knows how the work should be done, as was the habit with the ladies of olden time. A cook will not think the worse of her mistress if, instead of ringing the bell and scolding violently over an ill-cooked dinner, she descends to the kitchen and takes the pains to explain all the deficiencies of to-day, showing how they may be remedied to-morrow. And if this is done carefully and kindly, the chances are that they will be remedied; and a little temporary trouble will avoid endless trouble afterwards.

Fault-finding is inevitable; reproof, sharp and unmistakable, is sometimes necessary, nay, salutary; dismission, instant and sudden, without hope of reprieve or forgiveness, may occasionally be the only course possible; but no head of a household is justified in using towards any of its members one rough, or harsh, or contemptuous word. The mistress who scolds, and the master who swears at a servant, at once put themselves in a false position, sink from their true dignity, and deserve any impertinence they get.

"Impertinence!" I once heard remarked by a lady, a house-mother for many years, "why, I never had an impertinent word from a servant in my life."

Of course not, because in all her dealings with them she herself was scrupulously courteous—as courteous as she would have been to any of her equals, friends, or acquaintances. She had sense to see that, putting aside the duty of it, one of the chief differences between class and class, superior and inferior, educated and un-educated, is this unvarying politeness. I shall never forget watching an altercation between two London omnibus drivers—the one heaping on the other every opprobrious name he could think of; while his rival, sitting calmly on the box, listened in silence, then turned round to reply, "And you—you're a "—he paused, "you're a gentleman!" The satire cut sharp. Omnibus No. 1 drove away amidst shouts of laughter, mingled with hisses; omnibus No. 2 remained master of the field.

So, whatever may be the conduct of her servants, the "missis" loses her last hold over them if, however provoked, she allows them by any word or deed of hers to doubt that she is a lady.

And servants have a far keener appreciation of a "real lady," as they call it, than we give them credit for. They seldom fail to distinguish between the born gentlewoman, however poor, and the *nouveau riche*, whom only her riches make different from themselves. They are sharp enough to see that, as a rule, the born or educated gentlewoman, sure of herself and her position, will treat them much more familiarly and kindly than the other. And this kindness, even unaccompanied by tangible benefactions, what a powerful agent it is !

Of course, there are those whom we may emphatically term "the lower classes," who seem to consider the upper class not only their keepers, but their legitimate prey. But there are others, over whom gentleness of speech, thoughtfulness in word and act, a desire to save them trouble, a little pains taken to procure them some innocent pleasure, have a thousand times more influence than gifts, or even great benefits carelessly bestowed.

And here, among the duties of heads of families I would include one, too often overlooked, that of giving their servants a fair amount of actual pleasure. "All work and no play make Jack a dull boy," and the kitchen requires relaxation as well as the parlour. Not an occasional "day out," grudgingly given, and with a complete indifference as to where and how it is spent, but a certain amount of variety and amusement regularly provided.

The question is, what this should be; and there each individual family must decide for itself. I differ from that eloquent defender of servants' rights, who would put the pianoforte side by side with the dresser, and mix elegant literature with the cleaning of saucepans; but I do think that any servant with an ear for music or a taste for reading should be encouraged in every possible way that does not interfere with daily duty. " Work first, pleasure afterwards," should be the mistress's creed, for herself, her children, her servants; and she will generally find the work all the better done for not forgetting the pleasure.

Ignorance is at the root of half the errors of this world; errors which soon develop into actual sins. In spite of the not unfrequently given opinion that it is a mistake to educate our inferiors, and that the march of intellect of late years has been the cause of most of the evils from which we now suffer, I think it will always be found that the cleverer and better educated servants are, the greater help and comfort they prove in a household.

And oh, what a help, what a comfort! " Better is a friend that is near than a brother afar off," says Solomon. And often, in the cares, worries, and hard experiences of life, far better than even the friends outside the house are the faithful servants within it, who offer us no obtrusive sympathy, no well-meant yet utterly useless and troublesome advice, but simply do what we tell them, or know us well enough to do what we want without our telling; and by their regular mechanical ways make things smooth and comfortable about us, thereby creating an unconscious sense of repose amidst the sharpest trials. If I were to name the greatest domestic blessing that the mother of the family can have, next to a good and dutiful child, it is a faithful servant.

But, as I have said before, the blessing must be earned. And even in these days, it is in every one's power to earn it. Even if the present generation has so greatly deteriorated that a satisfactorily trained servant is almost impossible to find, there is always the raw material, the new generation, to work upon. Every mistress of a household, every clergyman of a parish, with other responsible agents who form the centre of a circle of dependants, may with a little pains keep their eyes upon all the growing-up girls and boys around them, catch them early, and guide them for good, in all sorts of practical ways. Of course this gives trouble—everything in life gives trouble ; it requires common sense and patience—qualities not too abundant in this world. But the thing can be done, and those who do it will rarely fail to reap the benefit. For it is one of those forms of charity which pays itself—" small profits and quick returns." And though this may be a mean reason to urge, just like the maxim that honesty is the best policy, still there are people in this world who will not be the less charitable for knowing that charity is a good investment.

It is especially so, when beginning at home it goes on to widen into the circles nearest home. There is a subject which has been well talked

over in public meetings, well discussed in news-
papers, for the last few years, yet remains pretty
nearly where it stood, when well-to-do people first
began to open their eyes to it—the condition of
the poor at their gates.

The question, Am I my brother's keeper? is
as serious to the rich man with regard to the
dependants outside his doors as within them.
This, setting aside the question of their spiritual
state. I do not hold with those who administer
tracts first and food afterwards; and I incline
to believe that the washing of the soul is very
useless until the body has been well treated with
soap and water. Each earnest man has his own
pet theory for dealing with the spiritual condition of those about him; but for their physical
state, so far as he can affect it, every man is
answerable.

Not in a large way. The great error of benevolent people nowadays is that they will
do everything largely. They begin far off,
instead of near at hand. They will subscribe
thousands of pounds for the famine in India,
the widows and orphans of a shipwreck or a

colliery accident, the presenting of a testimonial to the widow and children of some notable man, who in most cases ought to have himself provided for his belongings ; but the duty of seeing that the two or three families who depend on them have enough wages to live upon, a decent house to live in, and some kindly supervision and instruction to help them to live a sanitary and virtuous life, is far too small a thing for your great philanthropists.

Yet if they would manage to do this, and only this—just as every one in a large city is compelled to sweep the snow from his own doorstep—what an aggregate of advantage would be reached ! Each large household is a nucleus, round which gather, of necessity, several smaller ones. Coachman, groom, gardener, labourer, outdoor servants of every sort, must all trust for their subsistence to the great family. Thus, every man with an income of from one thousand to indefinite thousands per annum has inevitably a certain number, more or less, of human souls and bodies dependent on him for their well-being. Is he conscious of the responsibility? Does he recognise that in this, at least, he is his brother's keeper?

In large towns things are different. Though the poor hang festering upon the very robe's hem of the rich, and scarcely any grand street or square but has a wretched mews or back alley behind it, still the gulf between the two is so great that it is difficult to pass it. Then, too, the population is so migratory—here to-day, gone to-morrow—that any lasting influence is almost impossible. The evils only too possible—and rich neighbours would do well for their own sakes not to forget this—are the crimes that lurk, the diseases that breed, in these miserable, homeless homes.

Some people have been bold enough to attempt a remedy. Some noble, self-denying souls have gone from end to end of these courts and alleys, cleansing and reviving, pouring through them a wholesome stream of beneficence, which God grant may never run dry. For in our large cities this melancholy condition of things is inevitable. All honour be to them who attempt —not a cure, alas! but even an amelioration.

However in the country our landowners and large householders have no excuse for their sins. For years, ever since Charles Kingsley wrote his "Yeast," in which the noble girl, Argemone, dies of a fever caught at the miserable cottages which had been left year after year undrained, unrepaired, a hotbed of disease and contagion, the same thing has been going on in country villages, lovely and picturesque to the eye, but, if you look further, full of all things foul and vile. It is as bad or worse in new-built suburban neighbourhoods, where wealthy residents have been so anxious to drive uncomfortable neighbours away that there are literally no cottages. The mechanic has to go to his work, or the outdoor servant to his daily calling, miles and miles; and even then house accommodation is as wretched as it is limited; several families —not of the very poor, but of people able to pay for decent accommodation, if they could only get it—are huddled together in some ill-drained, ill-ventilated, and worse-built house, subdivided and sub-let to the last possibility.

As the neighbourhood increases, and with it

the absolute necessity for a certain number of
the poor to serve the rich, their need of house-
room increases too. So great is the press of
tenants, that rents rise; grasping builders run
up, on speculation, wretched strings of cottages,
bran new and taking on the outside—quite
"genteel residences" to look at—but within,
every conceivable want and abomination.
However bad great towns may be, anybody
who examines the dwelling-houses of—I will
not say the poor, but the working classes—in
the country, has good need to turn to all their
"brethren" who have money in hand, and ask
why, when building "palatial mansions" for
themselves, or even stately churches for—is it
for Him who expressly says He "dwells not in
houses made with hands"?—they cannot spare
a few hundred pounds to build a few decent cottages for their humbler neighbours? Simple, solid
cottages, where the wind does not whistle through
one-brick walls, nor the rain soak through
leaky windows, and the gaudy papering drop
off with damp; where water supply and house
drainage do not mingle—even as the respect-

able and the vile, the provident and the improvident, the sober and the drunkard, are often forced to mingle in these wretched homes. Consequently the best-intentioned helper, the most judicious friend, finds it difficult to choose between the bad and the good, the careful and the untidy, those who deserve to be aided and encouraged, and those whom any assistance makes only more helpless and more undeserving.

Nevertheless, we are still our brother's keeper. Not our seventeenth cousin—black, olive, or brown—but our brother who lives next door to us, and for whom we ought to do our very best before we go further. Therefore, I say, let every man sweep his own doorstep clean. Let him take a little trouble to use among his immediate dependants all the influence his position gives him. Let him try to make them good, if he can; but at any rate let him do his utmost to make them comfortable. I have heard it said that a thief is not half so likely to steal when he has got a clean shirt on; and I believe the master who takes pains to provide his servants with decent houses, safe from malaria, free from overcrowding—nay, who even condescends to look in and see that everything is neat and convenient, taking an interest in the papers on the walls and the flowers in the gardens—would soon cease to complain that they wasted or peculated his substance, or spent their own in the skittle-ground and the taproom.

But in this matter no absolute laws can be laid down, no minutiæ particularised. The subject is so wide, and each case must be judged on its own merits. Every man and woman must decide individually how far fortune has constituted them their brother's keeper, and to what extent they are fulfilling that trust. How it should be fulfilled they alone can tell. It lies between them and their consciences; or, to speak more solemnly, between them and their God.

"Those whom Thou hast given Me," said the divinest Master that ever walked this earth, of the men who instinctively called Him by that name. And though in this cynical generation it

may provoke a smile, the mere notion that our
hired servants, our followers and dependants,
are given to us by God that we may be His
agents in guiding and helping them, still
the fact, if it be a fact, remains the same,
whether we believe it or not. And I think it
would be a consolation at many a deathbed—
deathbeds watched and soothed by some long-
tried, faithful servant, and oftentimes only a
servant—to look back through the nearly ended
life upon a few waifs and strays rescued, a
few young souls guided in the right way, sufferers saved from worse suffering, honest "brothers" and sisters helped, strengthened, and
rewarded. The world may never know it, for
it is a kind of beneficence which does not show
outside; but I can imagine such a man or
woman—master or mistress—echoing without
any pride, but with a sort of thankful gladness,
the momentous words, "Those that Thou gavest
me I have kept : and none of them is lost."

Sermon VI. and Last.

GATHER UP THE FRAGMENTS.

VI.

I SHOULD premise of this sermon, that it is not a very cheerful one, nor meant for the very young. They, to whom joy seems as interminable as sorrow, at the time, will neither listen to it nor believe it. But their elders, who may have experienced its truth, and had strength to accept it as such, may find a certain calm even in its sadness. For these I write ; not those, until in their turn they have proved the same.

"Gather up the fragments which remain, that nothing be lost." So once said the Divine Master, after feeding His hungering five thousand. How often, even without relation to the circumstances under which they were first uttered, do the mere words flash across one's mind, in various crises of life; words full of deep meaning—solemn with pathetic warning.

For to how few has existence been anything like perfect, leaving no fragments to be gathered up? Who can say he has attained all his desires, fulfilled all his youth's promises? looks back on nothing he regrets, nor desires to add anything to what he has accomplished?

How many lives are, so to speak, mere relics of an ended feast, fragments which may be either left to waste, or be taken up and made the most of. For we cannot die just when we wish it, and because we wish it. The fact may be very unromantic, but it is a fact, that a too large dinner or a false step on the stairs kills much more easily than a great sorrow. Nature compels us to live on, even with broken hearts, as with lopped-off members. True, we are never quite the same again; never the complete human being; but we may still be a very respectable, healthy human being, capable of living out our threescore years and ten with tolerable comfort after all.

Of course this is very uninteresting. It is

not the creed of novels and romances. There everybody is happy and married, or unhappy and dies. A cynic might question whether, in his grand solution of all mundane difficulties, to transpose the adjectives, retaining the verbs, would not be much nearer the truth; since death ends our afflictions, and marriage very often begins them. But your cynics are the most narrow-visioned of all philosophers. Let them pass! Safer and better is it to believe that every one may, if he chooses, attain to a certain amount of happiness, enough to brighten life and make it, not only endurable, but nobly useful, until the end. But entire felicity is the lot of none, and moreover was never meant to be.

Until we have learnt to accept this fact reverently, humbly, not asking the why and wherefore, which we can never by any possibility find out; until then, our soul's education, the great purpose of our being in the body at all, is not even begun. We are still in the A B C of existence, and many a bitter tear shall we have to shed, many an angry fit of resistance to both lessons and Teacher, many a cruel craving after sunshiny play and delicious laziness, will be our portion, till we are advanced enough to understand why we are thus taught.

It is curious, if it were not so sad, to notice how many years of fruitful youth we spend less in learning than in wondering why we are compelled to learn, why we cannot be left to do just as we like, having everything to enjoy and nothing to suffer. For, whether we confess it or not, most of us start in life with the conviction that Providence somehow owes us a great debt of felicity, and if He does not pay it, there must be something radically wrong, not with ourselves, of course— in youth the last person we doubt is ourself— but with the whole management of the universe. "Here I am," the young man or maiden soliloquises. "I wish to be happy; it is Heaven's business to make me happy—me individually, without reference to the rest of the world, and whether or not I choose to obey the laws laid down for the general good. I am I: every blessing sent me I take as my right; every misfortune that befalls me is a cruelty or an injustice."

Odd as this reads, put so plainly, still I believe it is, if they will seriously examine themselves, the attitude that most young people take towards Providence, and the world in general, while they are still young.

A comfortable doctrine, but having one fault, in common with many other doctrines conceived out of the arrogant egotism of the human heart —it is not true.

"This God is our God," exclaims the Psalmist, adding, joyfully, "He will be our guide unto death." Ay, but He will also be the guide of millions more, equally His children, with whom we must take our lot; every minute portion of His creation being liable to be made subservient to the working of the whole. A working which, if not entirely by chance and for evil, must necessarily be by design, and for the general good of the whole. Any other theory of happiness strikes a blow at the root of all religious faith—the sense of a Divine Fatherhood, not

limited or personal, but unlimited and universal.

For it is God's relation to us, not ours to Him,
which is the vital question. The great craving
of humanity is—we want a God to believe in.
What He wants with us, or does with us, is a
secondary thing; being God, He is sure to do
right. I have sometimes smiled to hear deeply
religious people bless the Lord "for saving my
poor soul." Why, that is the very last thing
a creature, with a spark of His nature dwelling
in it, would dream of blessing Him for; or that
He would accept as a fit thanksgiving. Especially if that salvation involved, as it usually
does, the supposed condemnation of unknown
millions, including many dear friends of the
devout thanksgiver. That all religion should
consist merely in the saving of one's own individual soul! Such a creed is simply the carrying
out spiritually of that much-despised sentiment,
"self-preservation is the first law of nature;"
and the followers of it are as purely selfish as
the wrecked sailor, who, seizing for himself a
spar or a hencoop—nay, let us say at once, a

comfortable boat—calmly watches all his mates go down. For this, plainly put, is the position of many an earnest worshipper towards his self-invented God. But what a worshipper! and oh, not to speak it profanely, what a God!

You will perceive, this sermon is clearly "out of church," and would put me outside the pale of many churches. Not, I trust, outside that of the church invisible, spread silently over the whole visible world. Because "Gather up the fragments" is a text which it is useless for me to preach upon, or you to listen to, unless we both have a strong spiritual sense—a conviction of the nothingness of all things human, except those which bind the soul to its Maker, which we call religious faith. And though I am far from believing that the present world is nothing, and the world to come everything; that we are to console ourselves for every grief, and repay ourselves for every resignation, by the idea that thereby we somehow or other make God our debtor, ready to requite us in another existence for all we have lost, or wilfully thrown away, in this; still, it is hopeless either to teach or learn the difficult lesson, which, in plain words, I may call " making the best of things," without a firm trust, first in His love who bids us do it, secondly in our own duty of obedience to His paramount will, in great things and small, simply because it is His will, whether we understand it or not.

Therefore, I am no heretic, though I may say things that make orthodoxy shudder; perhaps because it has a secret fear that they may be true after all.

These " fragments " of lives—how they strew our daily path on every side! Not a house do we enter, not a company do we mix with, but we more than guess—we *know*—that these our friends, men and women, who go about the world, doing their work and taking their pleasure therein, all carry about with them a secret burden — of bitter disappointments, vanished hopes, unfulfilled ambitions, lost loves. Probably every one of them, when his or her smiling face vanishes from the circle, will change it into another, serious, anxious, sad—happy, if it be only sad, with no mingling of either bitterness or badness. That complete felicity, which the young believe in, and expect almost as a matter of certainty to come, never does come. Soon or late, we have to make up our minds to do without it; to take up the fragments of our blessings, thankful that we have what we have, and are what we are; above all that we have our own burden to bear, and not our neighbour's. But, whatever it is, we must bear it alone; and this gathering-up of fragments, which I am so earnestly advising, is also a thing which must be done alone.

The lesson is sometimes learnt very early. It is shrewdly said, "At three we love our mothers, at six our fathers, at twelve our holidays, at twenty our sweethearts, at thirty our wives, at forty our children, at fifty ourselves." Still, in one form or other, love is the groundwork of our existence.

So, at least, thinks the passionate boy or sentimental girl who has fallen under its influence. For I suppose we must all concede the everyday fact that most people fall in love some time or other, and that a good many do it even in their teens. You may call it "calf-love," and so it often is; and comes to the salutary end of such a passion—

> "Which does at once like paper set on fire,
> Burn—and expire."

But it gives a certain amount of pain and discomfort during the conflagration, and often leaves an ugly little heap of ashes behind.

Also, it is well to be cautious; as the foolishest of fancies may develop into a real love —the blessing or curse of a lifetime.

"Fond of her," I heard an old man once answer, as he stood watching his wife move slowly down their beautiful but rather lonely garden; they had buried eight of their nine children, and the ninth was going to be married that spring. "Fond of her?" with a gentle smile, "Why, I've been fond of her these fifty years!"

But such cases are very exceptional. It is so seldom that one love—a happy love—runs like a golden thread through the life of either man or woman, that we ought to be patient even with the most frantic boy, or forlorn girl, who has "fallen in love," and is enduring its first sharp pleasure—or pain—for both are much alike.

When they come and tell you that their hearts are broken, it is best not to laugh at them, but to help them to " gather up the fragments " as soon as possible. At first, of course, they will not agree that it is possible. " This or nothing ! " is the despairing cry; and though we may hint that the world is wide, and there may be in it other people, at least as good as the one particular idol, still we cannot expect them to believe it. Disappointed lovers would think it treason against love to suppose that life is to be henceforward anything than a total blank. It is so, sometimes; heaven knows! I confess to being one of those few who, in this age, dare still to believe in love, and in its awful influence, for good or for evil, at the very outset of life. But it is not the whole of life: nor ought to be.

The prevention of a so-called "imprudent" marriage—namely, an impecunious one—and the forcing on of another, which had nothing in the world to recommend it except money,

Q

has often been the ultimate ruin of a young
man, who would have been a good man,
had he been a happy man; had he married
the girl he loved. And in instances too numerous to count, have girls—through the common
but contemptible weakness of not knowing their
own minds, or the worse than weakness of being
governed by the minds of others in so exclusively a personal matter as marriage—driven
honest fellows into vice. Or else, into some
reckless, hasty union, whereby both the man
himself and the poor wife, whom he never
loved but only married, were made miserable
for life.

Generally speaking, men get over their love-
sorrows much easier than women. Naturally;
because life has for them many other things
besides love; for women, almost nothing. But
still one does find occasionally a man, pros-
perous and happy, kind to his wife, and devoted to his children, in whom the indelible
trace of some early disappointment is, that one
name is never mentioned, one set of associations entirely put aside. He is a good fellow

—a cheerful fellow too; he has taken up the fragments of his life and made the very best of them.   Yet, sometimes, you feel that the life would have been more complete, the cha- racter more nobly developed, if the man had had his heart's desire, and married his first love.

Which nobody does, they say; certainly, almost nobody; yet the world wags on; and everybody seems satisfied—at least, in public. Nay, possibly, in private too; for time has such infinite power of healing or hiding.   There is nothing harder than a lava stream grown cold.

Those of us who have reached middle age without dropping—who would ever drop?—the ties of our youth, move about encircled by dozens of such secret histories, forgotten by the outside world—half forgotten, perhaps, by the very actors therein—with whom we, the spectators, had once such deep sympathy.   Now, we sometimes turn and look at a face which we remember as a young face, alive with all the passion of youth—and we marvel to see how commonplace it has grown; reddening cosily over a good dinner, or sharp and eager over business greed; worn and wrinkled with nursery cares, or sweetly smiling in a grand drawing-room, ready to play its

> " Petty part,
> With a little hoard of maxims preaching down a daughter's heart."

A sort of gathering-up of fragments which those who are weak enough, or strong enough, still to believe in love, will think far worse than any scattering.

The young will not believe us when we tell them that their broken hearts may be mended; ought to be; since life is too precious a thing to be wasted over any one woman, or man either. It is given us to be made the most of; and this, whether we ourselves are happy or miserable. The misery will not last—the happiness will; if only in remembrance. No pure joy, however fleeting, contains any real bitterness, even when it is gone by.

But time only will teach this. At first there is nothing so overwhelming as the despair of youth, which sees neither before it nor behind;

refuses to be laughed out of, or preached out of, its cherished woe, which it deems a matter of conscience to believe eternal.

It will *not* be eternal; but best not to say so to the sufferer. Best to attempt neither argument nor consolation, only substitution. Hard work, close study, a sudden plunge into the serious business of life, that the victim may find the world contains other things besides love, is the wisest course to be suggested by those long-suffering, much-abused beings, parents and guardians. Love is the best thing—few deny that; but life contains many supplementary blessings too : honourable ambition, leading to a success well earned and well used; to say nothing of that calm strength which comes into a young man's heart when he has fought with and conquered fate, by first conquering himself, the most fatal fate of all.

Commonplace preaching this! Everybody has heard it. Strange, how seldom anybody thinks of acting upon it. In the temporary madness of disappointment a poor fellow will go and wreck his whole future; and when afterwards he would fain build up a new life—alas! there is no material left to build with.

Therefore, it is the duty of those older and wiser, who, perhaps, themselves have waded through the black river and landed safe on the opposite shore, to show him that it is not as deep as it seems, and that it has an opposite shore. He may swim through; with the aid of a stout heart and an honest self-respect; self-respect, not selfishness—for the most selfish creature alive is a young man in love, except towards the young woman he happens to be in love with. Not seldom, the very best lesson of life— bitter but wholesome—is taught to a young man by a love-disappointment.

Not so with women; they being in this matter passive, not active agents. So few girls are " in love " nowadays; so many set upon merely getting married, that I confess to a secret respect for any heart which has in it the capacity of being " broken." Not that it does break, unless the victim is too feeble physically to fight against her mental suffering; but the anguish is sore at the time. There is no cure for it, except one, suggested by a little girl I know, who with the innocent passion of six and a half adored a certain "beautiful Charlie" of nineteen. Some one suggested that Charlie would marry and cease to care for her. "Then I should be so unhappy," sighed the sad little voice.—"What, if he married a wife he was very fond of, and who made him quite happy—would you be unhappy then?"—"No!" was the answer, given after a slight pause, which showed this conclusion was not come to without thought. "No! I would love his wife, that's all."

The poor little maid had jumped by instinct—womanly instinct—to the true secret of faithful love—the love which desires, above all, the good of the beloved, and therefore learns to be brave enough to look at happiness through another's eyes.

This is the only way by which any girl can take up the fragments of a lost or unrequited affection; by teaching herself, not to forget it—that is impossible—but to rise above it; until the sting is taken out of her sorrow, and it becomes gradually transformed from a slow poison into a bitter but wholesome food.

Besides, though the suggestion may seem far below the attention of poetical people, there are such things as fathers and mothers, brothers and sisters, and other not undeserving relations, to whom a tithe of the affection wasted upon some (possibly) only half-deserving young man would be a priceless boon. And so long as the world endures there will always be abundance of helpless, sick, and sorrowful people calling on the sorrow-stricken one for aid, and ready to pay her back for all she condescends to give with that grateful affection which heals a wounded heart better than anything—except work.

Work, work, work! That is the grand pa-nacea for sorrow ; and, mercifully, there is no end of work to be done in this world, if anybody will do it. Few households are so perfect in their happy self-containedness that they are not glad oftentimes of the help of some lonely woman, to whom they also supply the sacred consolation of being able to help somebody, and thus perhaps save her from throwing herself blindly into some foolish career for which she has no real vocation, except that forced upon her by the sickly fancy of sorrow. For neither art, nor science, nor religion will really repay its votaries, if they take to it, like opium-eaters, merely to deaden despair.

And here I must own to a certain sympathy with those sisterhoods—yes, even Roman Catholic sisterhoods—who hold out pitying arms to sufferers like these; disappointed maidens, unhappy wives, childless widows; struck by some one of the many forms of incurable grief which are so common among women, whose destiny generally seems less to conquer than to endure. Of course, the natural duties, those which lie close at hand, are safest and best; but such do not come to all, and any duties are better than none; any work, even the painful and often revolting toil of a sister of charity, is safer than idleness.

For, say what you will, and pity them as you may, these broken hearts are exceedingly troublesome to the rest of the world. We do not like to see our relatives and friends going about with melancholy faces, perpetually weeping over the unburied corpse of some hopeless grief or unpardonable wrong. We had much rather they buried it quietly, and allowed us after a due season of sympathy to go on our way. Most of us prefer to be comfortable if we can. I have always found those the best liked people who have strength to bear their sorrows themselves, without troubling their neighbours. And the sight of all others most touching, most ennobling, is that of a man or woman whom we know to have suffered, perhaps to be suffering still, yet who still carries a cheerful face, is a burden to no friend, nor casts a shadow over any household—perhaps quite the contrary. Those whose own light is quenched are often the light-bringers.

To accept the inevitable; neither to struggle against it nor murmur at it, simply to bear it— this is the great lesson of life—above all to a woman. It may come late or early, and the learning of it is sure to be hard, but she will never be a really happy woman until she has learnt it. I have always thought two of the most pathetic pictures of women's lives ever given are Tennyson's "Dora"—

> "As time
> Went onwards, Mary took another mate :
> But Dora lived unmarried to her death,"

and Jeanie, in "Auld Robin Gray," who says, with the grave simplicity of a God-fearing Scotswoman—

> "I daurna think o' Jamie, for that wad be a sin ;
> So I will do my best a gude wife to be,
> For Auld Robin Gray is vera kind to me."

Besides lost loves, common to both men and women, there are griefs which belong perhaps to men only—lost ambitions. It is very sore for a man just touching, or having just pased, middle age, slowly to find out that he has failed in the promise of his youth; failed in everything— aspirations, hopes, actions—a man of whom strangers charitably say, "Poor fellow, there's a screw loose somewhere; he'll never get on in the world." And even his nearest friends begin mournfully to believe this ; they cease to hope, and content themselves in finding palliatives for a sort of patient despair. That "loose screw" —heaven knows what it is, or whether he himself is aware of it or not—always seems to prevent his succeeding in anything ; or else, without any fault of his own, circumstances have made him the wrong man in the wrong place, and it is too late now to get out of it. Pride and shame alike keep him silent ; yet he knows— and his friends know, and he knows they know it—that his career has been, and always will be, a dead failure; that the only thing left for him is to gather up the fragments of his vanished dreams, his lost ambitions, his wasted labours, and go on patiently to the end. He does so, working away at a business which he hates, or pursuing an art which he is conscious he has no talent for, or bound hand and foot in a mesh of circumstances against which he has not energy enough to struggle. Whatever form of destiny may have swamped him, he is swamped, and for life.

Yet even in a case like this, and there are few sadder, lies a certain consolation. People prate about heroes, but one sometimes sees a simple, commonplace man, with nothing either grand or clever about him, who, did we only know it, is more worthy the name of hero than many a conqueror of a city. Ay, though all the dream-palaces of his youth may have crumbled down ; or, like the Arabs, he may have had to build and live in a poor little hut under the ruins of temples that might have been. But One beyond us all knows the story of this pathetic " might-have-been," and has pity upon it—the pity that, unlike man's, wounds not, only strengthens and heals.

For, after all, patience is very strong. Making a mistake in the outset of life is like beginning to wind a skein of silk at the wrong end. It gives us infinite trouble, and perhaps is in a tangle half through, but it often gets smooth and straight before the close. Thus, many a man has so conquered himself, for duty's sake, that the work he originally hated, and therefore did ill, he gets in time to do well, and consequently to like. In the catalogue of success and failure, could such be ever truthfully written, it would be curious to note those who had succeeded in what they had no mind to, and failed in that which they considered their especial vocation. A man's vocation is that to which he is " called ; " only sometimes he mistakes the voice calling. But the voice of duty there is no mistaking, nor its response ; in the strong heart, the patient mind, the contented spirit,— especially the latter, which, while striving to the utmost against what is not inevitable, when once it is proved to be inevitable, accepts it as such, and struggles no more. Still, to do this requires not only human courage, but super-human faith ; the acknowledgment of a Will diviner than ours, to which we must submit, and in the mere act of submission find consolation and reparation.

This is above all necessary in the most irreparable shattering of any lot—an unhappy marriage. A subject so difficult, so delicate, that I would shrink from touching on it, were it not so terribly common, so mournfully true.

Yes ; optimists may deny, and pessimists exult in, the fact ; but I am afraid it is a fact— that few marriages are entirely happy. As few, perhaps, as those single lives which are proverbially supposed to be so miserable. This, because the average of people are, voluntarily or unvoluntarily, only too prone to be miserable; and those that are unhappy single, will not be cured by marriage, but will rather have the power of making two people wretched instead of one. Add to this, the exceeding rashness with which people plunge into a "state" which, as Juliet says—

" Well thou knowest is full of doubt and fear."

The wonder is, not that some married people are less happy than they hoped to be, but that any married people, out of the honeymoon, or even in it, are ever happy at all.

Also, it is curious to observe how many persons seem actually to enjoy misery; to throw away their good things, and fasten deliberately on their evil things; so that each day—instead of being a rejoicing over blessings that, possibly, are, like daily bread, only for the day—is wasted in dreary complainings; regrets for what is not, rather than thanksgivings for what is. It all springs from the strange idea before adverted to, that heaven is somehow our debtor for end-less felicity, which if we do not get, or, getting, waste and lose, we cry like Jonah over his withered gourd, "I do well to be angry."

As men do—no, not men; they are mostly silent, either from honour or pride—but women, when, having made a rash or loveless marriage, they wake up to find themselves utterly miser-able, and causing misery—all the sharper because it is irretrievable.

And yet that very irretrievableness is its best hope. Heretical as the doctrine may seem, I believe if one-half of the ordinary marriages one sees could have been broken without public scandal, they would have been broken, some-times even within the first twelve months. But the absolute inevitableness of the bond, at least in our English eyes, makes it fix itself like an iron band round a tree trunk—the very bark which it pierces grows over it in time. With the woman, at least; the man is rather different. But with both, if truly honourable men and women, having made a mistake in marriage, which was presumably a voluntary act, they

must abide by it till death. Death, that remorseless breaker of bonds—alike awful to contemplate by love or by hate. Since, I suppose,
the most brutally treated wife, the most heavily
bound and sorely tried husband, would never
contemplate that release without sensations
little short of those of a murderer.

You perceive I am not one of those who uphold
divorce. I believe that from no cause, except
that which the New Testament gives as a
reason for a man's putting away his wife, or a
woman her husband, should the tie be allowed to be broken ; at least, not so as to admit
of either party marrying another. The Catholic
Church is not far wrong in holding marriage
to be a sacrament, and its dissolution impossible ; though there are cases in which we must
admit the right—nay the necessity—of total
and life-long separation. But only in extreme
cases, and when to go on enduring hopeless
misery would sacrifice others beside the parties
themselves. These two, undoubtedly, alas ! fall
under the lash of that grim truth, " If you make
your own bed, you must lie upon it."

And is it not sad—if it were not often so heroic—the way people do lie on it? with the iron spikes eating into their very flesh; making no complaint, keeping a fair outside to the world, and telling heaps of innocent lies, which deceive nobody, except perhaps those who tell them.

A perfect marriage is as rare as a perfect love. Could it be otherwise, when both men and women are so imperfect? Could aught else be expected? Yet all do expect it. Does not every young couple married believe they are stepping from the church door into entire felicity, to end only with their lives? Yet, look at them ten, fifteen, twenty years after, and how have those lives turned out? Should some old friend pay them a visit, will he or she return, envying their felicity, as perhaps on that wedding morning; or hugging themselves in their own independent old-bachelorship, or peaceful old-maidism, thinking happiness is, after all, a much more equally spread thing than they once supposed?

So it is. Though, according to the old joke,

married people are often like little boys bathing,
who cry with chattering teeth to the boys on
the shore, "Do come in, it's *so* warm,"—it is
not always warm. There is no sadder picture—
if it were not such an everyday picture—than
two young people, married perhaps for love,
at any rate for liking, but married in haste, to
repent at leisure; which they piteously do.
Knowing little or nothing of each other's temper, taste, character, they slowly wake up to
find these so diverse, that it was morally impossible they could have been happy, for very
long; and here they are, tied together, in the
most intimate union that life allows, *for ever.*
A thought absolutely maddening;—at first, and
with people of sensitive or impulsive natures.
I fear, if we could look into our neighbours'
hearts, the catalogue of suicides never committed, of elopements unaccomplished, even
of unperpetrated murders, would be, to those
who see no difference between the thought and
the act—something startling, nay, appalling.

But these tragedies do not happen—at least,
not often. They drop into "genteel comedy."

" Can two walk together, unless they be agreed?"
Very many couples are not "agreed," far from
it ; yet seeing they must walk together somehow, they make up their minds to do it, and
they *do* do it. Ay, in spite of good-natured
friends, who cannot help observing how unhappy
they are, and perhaps how happy they might both
have been if each had been married to a different sort of person. But this is not the case :
they are married to the person whom they
themselves chose, or fate chose for them. The
thing is done, and there is no undoing it.

None ; for the unavoidable bigamies and innocent adulteries so popular nowadays are to all
right-minded, I will not even say Christian
people, actual sin ; simple, absolute, inexcusable
sin. No nonsense about " elective affinities "
and " platonic friendships " can excuse the smallest trifling with the sanctity of the marriage bond.
The empty heart must remain empty for ever.

Yet it is pitiful—most pitiful! especially if
the couple are not bad, only ill-assorted, and
young still; young enough to make a possible future of twenty or thirty years look so

black in the distance! haunted by the pale
phantom of dead love, the wretched will-o'-
the-wisp of a lost happiness. God help them,
poor souls! No wonder such a lot should drive
men wicked, and women mad; as it does, oftener
perhaps than the world knows.

For such a grief is of necessity a secret one.
The husband pays all outward respect to his
silly, bad-tempered wife; the wife hides all her
husband's faults and exalts his virtues. Both do
their best to take up the fragments that remain,
pretending all is exactly as they desire; throwing dust in their neighbours' eyes; and, partly
from pride, partly from shame, sometimes from
mere worldly prudence, keeping up appearances
before the world. Whatever the motive, it
answers the purpose—a righteous purpose too.
Society is not scandalized, the home is not
broken up, friends and kindred are not troubled.
They only guess; they really know nothing.
And if guessing something, they look on in
compassionate sympathy: they attempt no help
or advice, for none is asked; it would be rather
resented than not. The fragments must be

gathered up alone, by each forlorn sufferer, out of the depths of the suffering heart. And how?

It is a curious opposite picture to our vaunted English "love" marriages that the French "arranged" marriages often turn out so well. The reason is apparent. Two people cannot live long together in indifference. The tie between a married pair, howsoever married, must be one of either love or hate; and, being an indissoluble tie—also, few people being wholly wicked or entirely detestable—the chances are that in time it becomes the former. One by one they discover each other's virtues, and learn to be tender over each other's faults. Having, unlike lovers, only the future to deal with, no dead past to bury out of sight, they are kinder to one another even than those who were once much more than kind. For there is no injustice deeper than the conscience-stricken injustice of a waning love—no cruelty sharper than that of apostates to a forsaken idol. And it might be a nice question for some modern Court of Love to decide—which is the bitterest lot, to cling through life to a love unfulfilled, or to have attained one's heart's desire, and found the object not worth possessing?

Nevertheless, the saving fact which I have acknowledged and accounted for concerning these "mariages de convenance," which we in England condemn so much, gives a hope for those almost more hopeless "love" marriages, which, beginning so brightly, sink slowly into permanent gloom, and end—who knows how?—unless there come to the rescue that "stern daughter of the voice of God"—Duty— which is still "loved of love," and has often- times the power to revive love, even when to all outward eyes it is dead for ever.

Duty—pure duty—without any thought of personal reward or personal happiness—is the strongest, sweetest, most sacred force that do- mestic life possesses. And it brings with it its own consolations; not perhaps *the* consolation it craves—it is strange how seldom heaven gives us poor mortals exactly what we desire—but something else, in substitution. How many a sorrowful woman heals her bruised heart beside

her baby's cradle! How many a disappointed,
lonely man—to whom his wife is no companion
and no helpmeet—takes comfort in his baby
daughter, and looks forward hopefully to the
time when she will be a grown woman; his
friend and solace, the sharer of his tastes and
humourer of his innocent hobbies—all, in short,
that her mother might have been, but is not!
Yet he will not love her mother the less, but
rather the more, for the child's sake.

He is right, and the forlorn woman is right,
who, having missed the highest bliss, has
strength to take up the fragments of a secondary
one; so that, in the divine and comforting words
before referred to, "nothing be lost." If she
has children, she loves them, often passionately;
not alas! for the father's sake; but they teach
her to be patient with the father for the sake of
his children. While the man who, however inferior his wife may be—and, the glamour of
passion ended, he knows her to be, and knows
that all the world knows it too—never allows
her to suffer for his own rash mistake, but pays
her all tender respect as the mistress of his

house and the mother of his offspring—that
man, who, whatever his inward sufferings, be-
trays nothing, and makes no one miserable but
himself, will have at least the peace of a quiet
conscience. As he goes about the world, doing
his duty therein, with a calm brow and a reti-
cent tongue—whatever people suspect, be sure
they will say nothing. He has accepted his lot,
taken up his burden ; and will carry it through
life, steadily, nobly, uncomplainingly. Therefore, man will honour him, and God will sustain
him—to the end.

Also, burdens lighten—or else the back gets
used to them by degrees. How many a house
do we enter, and witnessing its secret cares,
think—not without thankfulness—that we can
bear our own troubles, but we could *not* bear
theirs. Yet we see they are borne, even with
apparent unconsciousness, by those accustomed
to them. The endless snarling and pitiless
fault-finding of a bad-tempered man passes harm-
lessly over his placid, brave-hearted wife ; the
intolerable silliness, or churlishness, or selfishness of one member of a family is perhaps

hardly noticed by the rest. We have all so much to put up with from other people—and other people the same, or worse, from us—that even love itself will not stand upright, unless it has the strong backbone of duty to keep it upright. That is (if I can put it clearly without falling into cant phraseology) unless in great things and small we are guided by a motive below and above ourselves and our personal interests ; unless, in short, every love we have is made subservient to the love of God.

If this be so, surely it is possible, even after shipwrecks like these, not to let ourselves drift away into a sea of despair. The vessel has gone down, but there may be a little boat somewhere ; our sail may be torn to ribbons, but we have oars still ; if we cannot row, perhaps we can swim. Somehow or other we may touch land.

But there is one wreck in which the sufferers can never touch land, unless it be the Land Eternal—I mean the fate of those who find themselves smitten with incurable disease, or doomed to hopeless invalidism. It may be exalting matter over mind, placing the physical above the spiritual, but I think to be imprisoned for life in a miserable body which hampers and paralyzes the soul is as sad a lot as any of the sentimental sorrows which are here chronicled. The more so as it is such an every-day occurrence that it excites little compassion.

We lavish great sympathy upon sudden, accidental illnesses; but the chronic sufferers, those who carry about with them some perpetual pain, for which there is no ease but death; or even the mere valetudinarians, who "never feel quite well," cannot do things which other people do, and have continually to give up things they would like to do, for fear of being a trouble to others—these we get so used to that we often cease to pity them, or to consider what a heavy burden they have to bear, and how much courage they need in order to sustain it at all.

For it is such an essentially solitary burden. No healthy person can understand even the small misery of feeling "always tired;" and when it comes to worse than this, when one has to sit still and gaze into long years of helplessness,

perhaps acute pain, and, though it is still noon-
day, face the certainty that no genial sun will
ever burst into that dim twilight—then life grows
very difficult, very dark. To most, the future is
so obscure that they can build it up in any
fanciful way they please; but to these it is like a
blank wall with nothing beyond. To sit down and
face it, knowing that our small round of interests,
pleasures, or labours can never be wider than
now, nay, will probably narrow day by day;
that we can give no pleasure to anybody, and
receive little from anybody; that, somehow or
other, we know not why, God has made us
separate from our kind; to invent a poor
fragmentary life for ourselves, and bear it by
ourselves, until death comes to untie the knot
and lift off the burden—this, I think, is as sad a
fate as can befall any human being.

The only way to meet it is that which I have
already counselled in other but scarcely sharper
sorrows. Accept it. Cease trying to get well,
and worrying about each small symptom of
being worse or better. Remember Hezekiah,
who " sought not the Lord, but the physicians."

Not that I defend the Peculiar People, who hold that prayers are to supersede mustard plaisters, and esteem anointing with oil a substitute for good food and wholesome water. Still I do think there is something in the solemn peace of a soul that has ceased to struggle with its body, but takes cheerfully the modicum of health allowed it, which actually conduces to that very health which is resigned.

When once an invalid has strength to say, "It does not much matter; at worst I can but die," sickness and death itself lose their terrors. An old man, a cruel sufferer, once said to me, "If my pain is tolerable, I must bear it; if it is intolerable, I shall not have to bear it long." Nor had he; and when, not many days after, I stood looking down on the peaceful face, so grand in its everlasting calm, with the wrinkles all smoothed out, and the irritable contractions of pain for ever gone, I wished that to the end of my days I might have strength to remember those words.

Remember them, too, you whose life is but the fragments of what it might have been, either in

mind or body—for the mind is so strangely
affected by the body. Yet try to gather up these
fragments : they may be worth something still.
Try to separate the spiritual from the physical
as much as you can, and when you grow irritable, exacting, prone to see everything in an
exaggerated light, and to think that never was
any one so afflicted as you, say to yourself, " It
is only my body ; I, the real me, must not let it
conquer me. This flesh is my temporary dun-
geon, yet—

> " Stone walls do not a prison make,
> Nor iron bars a cage "—

the ' mind innocent and quiet ' may abide with
me still."

Ay, and so it often is. Are not some of the
very sweetest faces we know, faces that memory
falls back upon and recalls in the tumult of life
with a sense of rest and peace, those of confirmed invalids, who may have spent years of
such imprisoment, perhaps only moving from
bed to sofa, and back to bed ; well aware that
they never will move elsewhere except to the
one narrow couch where we all must lie, yet

never complaining, never craving after the outside world, which circles noisily round their perpetual silence; exacting no sympathy,—on the contrary, giving it to all and any who need.

"I have no troubles," said, smiling, one of those sweet saints, whom most people would have considered "a great martyr." "It is you others who come to me with all yours."

So we do, we who are still in the thick of the fight; to these, who seem as if their battle were done for ever. How often do we find counsel and comfort by the couch of some dear woman —it is generally a woman—whom the world calls "a terrible sufferer," but whose sufferings are the last thing she talks about. She has let herself go, and is absorbed in the interests of other people. The fragments of her life that remain to her she has made so beautiful, that you almost forget it was ever meant to be, like other lives, a perfect whole; that the wasted frame before you was ever a merry baby, a happy girl, a young woman looking forward to woman's natural destiny. All that is over, yet she is not unhappy; nay, she is actually happy, in her own way; no one could look in her face and doubt it. But it is a happiness quite different from and beyond ours; something which naught earthly can either give or take away.

This is a bright picture, which I would fain place opposite to the dark pictures I have drawn, compromising nothing and denying nothing; yet saying after all, "Take courage. God never leaves Himself without a witness. In the deepest darkness is a possibility of light."

For there is that in the human soul which *will not* die. Neither mental nor physical suffering will kill it before its time. And neither will extinguish in it the germ of possible happiness, in this world at least; whether or not in other worlds, God knows. But He has said enough to prove to us two things—that here on earth sin is the only absolute death, and "Deliver us from evil" the only true salvation.

Therefore, mere pain, in all forms, becomes a temporary and endurable thing, if we will only try to see it as such, accustoming our eyes to behold the good rather than the bad; choosing in our daily life to eat the food and reject the poison.

Easy enough, one would say, yet nobody does it. People sit and mourn over the fragments of their scattered joys, blind to the blessings they have, seeking madly for blessings denied. The rich complain of their responsibilities, the poor of their renunciations. The single think they would have been happy married; the married reply warningly, "Keep as you are." Many-childed parents groan under the burden of that bright troop of boys and girls, whom some empty household longs enviously for, with an angry protest against Providence, whose gifts are so unequally divided. Nobody will see his own blessings, or open his heart to enjoy them, till the golden hour has gone by for ever, and he finds out too late all that he might have had and might have been.

A discovery, made sometimes in an empty room or by a graveside, knowing that all the tears in the world will never lift that stone or fill that vacant chair; that all our ceaseless complainings, our angry fault-findings, even our

S

real wrongs, sink into nothing before the remorseless stillness of death. Even if life were not the absolute whole we expected it to be, if our friends were not perfect, nor ourselves either, why did we fall into despair, instead of quietly setting to work to gather up the fragments that remained, suffering nothing to be lost? Now, we never can gather them up any more. The great Destroyer has passed by, and there they lie—must lie—for ever.

Gather up the fragments. In every human life there are sure to be some. Every one of us has a secret chamber somewhere, filled with inhabitants whom none but himself can see; it rests with himself alone whether they shall be decaying corpses or only beautiful ghosts.

"God made me what I am, and made my lot what He willed it to be," is a truth not inconsistent with the other truth, that He gives us the materials to work with, but leaves the workmanship in our own hands. Every man can make or mar his own life; at any rate, it appears so. The fact that we know nothing of the results of our acts, makes them, as regards ourselves, absolutely independent; and the impossibility of gazing one inch into the impenetrable future comes to the same thing as if we beheld it all.

> " Lead Thou me on : I do not ask to see
> The distant scene : one step 's enough for me."

But that one step must be taken steadily, firmly, religiously. There must be no looking back, no mourning over the inexorable past. Each day —such a little day, and every one circling round so quietly that they mount into weeks, and months, and years, before we know what we have lost or gained!—each day must be filled up, minute by minute, with those duties which are in themselves joys, or grow to be. If among them ever rises the spectral face of the never-forgotten might-have-been — beautiful in its eternal youth, perfect in its unattained felicity— why fear? It is but a ghost, and life is a reality.

Ay, a useful, useable, noble reality. Happy, too, when once the grim idol Self has been dethroned for ever. For it is a truth which we all have to learn—oftentimes through many a bitter lesson—that we never can be happy until we cease trying to make ourselves so.

I said that this would be a rather sad sermon, to the young; but it is not so sad as it seems. There comes a time—to some earlier, to others later—when faith has to take the place of hope, and better even than bliss is consolation. Surely, then, it is something to know, on looking round on those about us, men and women, that the lives which seem the most complete—that is, have most perfectly fulfilled the end for which they were given—are very seldom what we call "fortunate" lives. Few have been carried out exactly as they began; fewer still have attained the felicity they expected. Some—and those often the noblest and highest—have been saddened by one or other of those secret, silent tragedies which are always happening around us, which we all know, or at least guess at, but never speak of; nor do they.

I once knew a dear old lady—so sweet, so bright, so clever; wearing her eighty years "as lightly as a flower." When you talked with her you would have thought her a woman of thirty, so full was she of all the quick sympathy of youth, the wise tenderness of middle age. Of the weaknesses of old age she had absolutely none. Her interest in all those about her was such that she never seemed to think of herself at all. No complaint, no murmur at her own ailments—and she had ailments, and sorrows too—ever fell from her lips; her only anxiety was about the cares of other people, and how she could lighten them, in great things and small. Her bounty knew no limits except her means, which were not great; "but," she once said, smiling, "I need so little; and then you see, my dear, I always pay my bills every week, so as to give no trouble to anybody afterwards." Thus she kept house, with the utmost order, yet with ceaseless hospitality. It was indeed the House Beautiful, to whose gates all who came departed refreshed and strengthened, and whence no creature who came in want or grief was ever sent empty away.

I need not name it; many now living will remember it; and none who were familiar there could ever forget it, or her, as she sat in her quiet corner, with her sweet old face, and her lovely little ringed hands—peaceful, idle hands; since for some years before she died she was nearly blind.   Yet her blindness, though, coming so late in life, it made her very helpless, never made her sad or dull; she could still listen to and join in conversation, and she greatly liked society, especially that of the young.   There was always a tribe of young people coming about her, telling her all their doings and plannings, their amusements and their troubles.   She was fond of them, and they —they adored her!   One girl in particular, owned that the first time this dear old lady voluntarily kissed her, she felt "as if she had been kissed by her first love."

When she died—at over eighty, certainly, but her executors had to guess at the date, for she was an old maid, without any near relations, and had often said she did not even know her own age, it was so long since she was born— when she died there was found among her private papers a portrait of a young man in a foreign military dress.   No one could guess who it was; the name—there was a name—no one had ever heard of. At last some old acquaintance recalled a far-away tradition of her having been once about to be married; somehow the marriage was broken off, but the two remained friends, and, it was believed, corresponded and occasionally met, till his death, which happened when she was about fifty years old. For his nephew—and heir, he having died unmarried—had then been to see her; somebody recollected having met the young man at her house, and her introducing him by name. After that name on the miniature all was silence. She was never heard to name the name again. Yet she lived on for thirty more years.

"What do you do when you are quite alone?" was once asked anxiously of her, when she was too blind either to write, or sew, or read.

"What do I do? My dear, I sit and think. I have so much to think about—and so many."

"And are you never dull?"

"Dull? Oh, no! I am quite happy."

She was, I am sure. You could see it in her face; the peaceful happiness of a soul which has ceased to " bother itself" about itself at all, and is absorbed in kindly cares for other people. Her last act—the last time she ever crossed her threshold—was, I remember, a visit of kindness, partly as an excuse to take for a drive a person who was too feeble to walk much. She was then extremely feeble herself; and, climbing a steep stair, one who assisted her said anxiously, " I fear you are very tired?" "Yes," she replied, "I am always tired now. But," turning suddenly round with the brightest of smiles, "never mind; it will be all right soon." Four weeks after she lay in her final rest, looking so young, so pretty, so content; that those who best loved her choked down their sobs and smiled, saying, " It was like putting a baby to sleep."

This is but one story out of many which I could tell, even out of my own knowledge, to prove that the fragments of a broken life can be so gathered up as to make a noble and even a happy life unto the end. Many a time, as we go on our troublous way through the world, are we cheered and encouraged by the sight of such ; old men who have done their work, and for whom is come the time of rest; the " blind man's holiday" between the lights, when they do nothing, and nobody expects them to do anything but look back on the fruits of their labour and rejoice ; old women who have their children around them, and grandchildren, in whom they take over again all a mother's delight freed from a mother's anxiety. Lastly—and these are not the least numerous, and perhaps the most touching of all—unmarried women, whose lives must necessarily have been incomplete, barren of joy, or clouded with incurable grief; yet one has but to look on their faces, sweet and saintly, to perceive that their evil has brought forth good— that, whatever their own lot may have been, to others they have proved a continual blessing. How can those fail to be blessed, who are everybody's comfort and everybody's help ?

Occasionally, too, we meet persons, still in middle age, for whom, it is easy to see, the sun has gone down at noon. Something has happened—we know not what, or perhaps we do know, but never mention it—something which will make their future like that of a tree with its "leader" broken; it may not die, it may grow up green and strong, but it will never grow tall, it will never be a perfect tree. With them, too, life in its highest sense is over; the play is played out — the feast is ended; there is nothing left but to gather up the fragments and endure.

And they are gathered. Slowly, painfully may be, but it is done. Nothing is lost. Nothing remains to cumber, corrupt, or decay. Everything available to use still, is used—strength, talents, energies, affections; all that God gave has been given back to Him; not perhaps in the way the offerer once desired to give it, but nevertheless in the right way, as the final result proves. And He has accepted the sacrifice; and requited it, too. Not perhaps with earthly felicity; not at all with the sort of felicity longed for; but with something better than happiness—peace; that peace which one sees sometimes on very suffering faces—it was seen continually on the dear old face I have spoken of—"the peace of God which passeth all understanding."

There is a psalm of David—poor King David, who paid so dearly in sorrow for every sin he committed, yet who had strength over and over again to gather up the fragments of his piteous errorful life, and live on—ay, and to die in faith, and in hope of his never-builded temple; there is a psalm, I say, in which he speaks of those who "have their portion in this life." He never blames them; he envies them not. Neither does he murmur at the will of God, who sees fit to fill them with His "hid treasure," and to give them the Jew's crowning blessing, "children at their desire;" that they may "leave the rest of their substance for their babes."

"But as for me," he continues, and you can almost hear the ringing of the triumphant harp —"David's harp of solemn sound"—"as for me, I will behold Thy presence in righteousness; and when I awake up after Thy likeness I shall be satisfied with it."

Thoroughly "satisfied." Nothing lost. Nothing scattered or wasted. No fragments to be gathered up; everything perfect and complete in Him—in the fulness of Him which filleth all in all.

May it one day be so with us, my brethren and sisters! Amen.

*   *   *   *   *

These Sermons out of Church are ended.

THE END.

Works by Augustus J. C. Hare.

I.
MEMORIALS OF A QUIET LIFE.

With 2 Steel Portraits.   Twelfth Edition.   2 vols. crown 8vo, 21s.

"This is one of those books which it is impossible to read without pleasure. It conveys a sense of repose not unlike that which everybody must have felt out of service-time in quiet little village churches.   Its editor will receive the hearty thanks of every cultivated reader for these profoundly-interesting 'Memorials' of two brothers, whose names and labours their universities and their Church have equal reason to cherish with affection and remember with pride, who have smoothed the path of faith to so many troubled wayfarers, strengthening the weary and confirming the weak."—*Standard*.

II.
DAYS NEAR ROME.

With more than 100 Illustrations by the Author.

Second Edition.   2 vols. crown 8vo, 24s.

"Henceforward it must take its place as a standard work indispensable to every intellectual student."—*Times*.
"A delightful sequel to Mr. Hare's 'Walks in Rome.'"—*Spectator*.
"The amount of information crowded into these two delightful volumes is simply marvellous."—*Hour*.

III.
WALKS IN ROME.

Fourth Edition.   2 vols. crown 8vo, 21s.

"The best handbook of the city and environs of Rome ever published. . . . . It cannot be too much commended."—*Pall Mall Gazette*.

IV.
WANDERINGS IN SPAIN.

With Illustrations by the Author.   Third Edition.   Crown 8vo, 10s. 6d.

"Here is the ideal book of travel in Spain, which exactly anticipates the requirements of everybody who is fortunate enough to be going to that enchanted land, and which ably consoles those who are not so happy, by supplying the imagination from the daintiest and most delicious of its stores."—*Spectator*.

Uniform with "Memorials of a Quiet Life."
THE ALTON SERMONS.

By the late AUGUSTUS WILLIAM HARE.   Crown 8vo, 10s. 6d.

"Sermons which have taken their place with English classics, which were understood and liked by rustics when delivered in the tiny village church, and when printed were read and admired by the most learned and fastidious."—*Nonconformist*.

DALDY, ISBISTER, & CO., 56, LUDGATE HILL, E.C.

Annals of a Quiet Neighbourhood.
Fifth Thousand. Crown 8vo, 6s.

The Seaboard Parish.
Third Thousand. Crown 8vo, 6s.

Wilfrid Cumbermede.
Third Thousand. Crown 8vo, 6s.

Unspoken Sermons.
Sixth Thousand. Crown 8vo, 3s. 6d.

The Miracles of Our Lord.
Second Thousand. Crown 8vo, 5s.

Works of Fancy and Imagination:
Being a Reprint of Poetical and other Works. Pocket-volume Edition, in neat case, £2 2s.

* *The Volumes are sold Separately in plain cloth at 2s. 6d. each.*

At the Back of the North Wind.
With Illustrations by Arthur Hughes. Third Thousand. Crown 8vo, cloth gilt extra, 5s.

Ranald Bannerman's Boyhood.
With Illustrations by Arthur Hughes. Second Thousand. Crown 8vo, cloth extra, 5s.

The Princess and the Goblin.
With Illustrations. Third Thousand. Crown 8vo, cloth gilt extra, 5s.

Dealings with the Fairies.
With Illustrations by Arthur Hughes. Sixth Thousand. Square 32mo, cloth gilt extra, 2s. 6d.

DALDY, ISBISTER, & CO., 56, LUDGATE HILL, E.C.